The Newbery Medal

The Newbery Medal, the first award of its kind, is the official recognition by the American Library Association of the most distinguished children's book published during the previous year. It is the primary and best known award in the field of children's literature.

Frederic G. Melcher first proposed the award, to be named after the eighteenth-century English bookseller John Newbery, to the Children's Librarian Section of the American Library Association meeting on June 21, 1921. His proposal was met with enthusiastic acceptance and was officially adopted by the ALA Executive Board in 1922. The award itself was commissioned by Mr. Melcher to be created by the artist Rene Paul Chambellan.

Melcher's formal agreement with the ALA Board included the following statement of purpose: "To encourage original creative work in the field of books for children. To emphasize to the public that contributions to the literature for children deserve similar recognition to poetry, plays, or novels. To give those librarians, who make it their life work to serve children's reading interests, an opportunity to encourage good writing in this field."

The medal is awarded by the Association for Library Service to Children, a division of the ALA. Other books on the final ballot for the Newbery are considered Newbery Honor Books.

In evaluating the candidates for exceptional children's literature, the committee members must consider the following criteria:

- The interpretation of the theme or concept
- Presentation of the information, including accuracy, clarity, and organization
- Development of plot
- Delineation of characters
- Delineation of setting
- Appropriateness of style
- Excellence of presentation for a child audience
- The book as a contribution to literature as a whole. The committee is to base its decision primarily on the text of the book, although other aspects of a book, such as illustrations or overall design, may be considered if they are an integral part of the story being conveyed.

Titles in

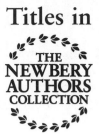

THE NEWBERY AUTHORS COLLECTION

For the Sake of Freedom
and Other Selections by Newbery Authors

The Highest Hit
and Other Selections by Newbery Authors

The Horse of the War God
and Other Selections by Newbery Authors

Lighthouse Island
and Other Selections by Newbery Authors

Dancing Tom
and Other Selections by Newbery Authors

Adoniram
and Other Selections by Newbery Authors

Dancing Tom

and Other Selections by Newbery Authors

Edited by Martin H. Greenberg
and Charles G. Waugh

Gareth Stevens Publishing
A WORLD ALMANAC EDUCATION GROUP COMPANY

The American Library Association receives a portion of the sale price of each volume in *The Newbery Authors Collection.*

The Newbery Medal was named for eighteenth-century British bookseller John Newbery. It is awarded annually by the Association for Library Service to Children, a division of the American Library Association, to the author of the most distinguished contribution to American literature for children. The American Library Association has granted the use of the Newbery name.

A note from the editors: These stories reflect many of the values, opinions, and standards of language that existed during the times in which the works were written. Much of the language is also a reflection of the personalities and lifestyles of the stories' narrators and characters. Readers today may strongly disagree, for example, with the ways in which members of various groups, such as women or ethnic minorities, are described. In compiling these works, however, we felt that it was important to capture as much of the flavor and character of the original stories as we could. Rather than delete or alter language that is intrinsically important to the literature, we hope that these stories will give parents, educators, and young readers a chance to think and talk about the many ways in which people lead their lives, view the world, and express their feelings about what they have lived through.

Please visit our web site at: www.garethstevens.com
For a free color catalog describing Gareth Stevens Publishing's list of high-quality books and multimedia programs, call 1-800-542-2595 (USA) or 1-800-461-9120 (Canada). Gareth Stevens Publishing's Fax: (414) 332-3567.

Library of Congress Cataloging-in-Publication Data available upon request from publisher. Fax: (414) 336-0157 for the attention of the Publishing Records Department.

ISBN 0-8368-2859-3

First published in 2001 by
Gareth Stevens Publishing
A World Almanac Education Group Company
330 West Olive Street, Suite 100
Milwaukee, WI 53212 USA

Dancing Tom by Elizabeth Coatsworth. Copyright © 1938 by Elizabeth Coatsworth. Reprinted by permission of the executrix for the author's estate, Kate Barnes.

"Death of Red Peril" by Walter D. Edmonds. Copyright © 1928 by Walter D. Edmonds. First published in *The Atlantic Monthly.* Reprinted by permission of the author and his agent, Harold Ober Associates.

"Down from the Hills" by Lois Lenski. Copyright © 1968 by Lois Lenski. Reprinted by permission of the executor for the Lois Lenski Covey Foundation, Moses & Singer, LLP.

"Mary Silver" by Elizabeth Coatsworth. Copyright © 1935 by The Methodist Book Concern. Reprinted by permission of the executrix for the author's estate, Kate Barnes.

"Once in the Year" by Elizabeth Yates. Copyright © 1991 by Upper Room Books. Reprinted by permission of the author.

"Once a Cowboy" by Will James. Copyright © 1951 by Will James. Reprinted by permission of the Will James Art Company, Billings, Montana.

"The Familiar Path" by Lois Lenski. Copyright © 1963 by Lois Lenski. Excerpted from chapters 1, 2, and 3 of *Shoo-Fly Girl.* Reprinted by permission of the executor for the Lois Lenski Covey Foundation, Moses & Singer, LLP.

Cover illustration: Joel Bucaro

Printed in the United States of America

1 2 3 4 5 6 7 8 9 05 04 03 02 01

❧ Contents ❧

Edited by Martin H. Greenberg and Charles G. Waugh

Dancing Tom
by Elizabeth Coatsworth 7

Death of Red Peril
by Walter D. Edmonds 18

Down from the Hills
by Lois Lenski 33

Mary Silver
by Elizabeth Coatsworth 49

Once in the Year
by Elizabeth Yates 64

A Tale of the Poplar
by Charles Boardman Hawes 74

Once a Cowboy
by Will James 83

The Familiar Path
by Lois Lenski 101

Author Biographies 147

Newbery Award-Winning Books 151

Dancing Tom

Elizabeth Coatsworth

Nearly a hundred years ago there lived on the upper Ohio a man, a woman and a baby boy. The man's name was Caleb Foster and his wife's name was Jenny. The little boy, who was only a year old, was called John. They lived in a log house which Caleb had built himself, and all about them was the land Caleb had cleared with the help of Lion, the yellow ox, and Tiger, the brindle one.

There he planted corn and beans and rye, but his hay came from the wild meadows near the river. Caleb and Jenny were young and strong. He cut down trees, split fence rails, plowed, hoed, and built, hunted and trapped. She cooked and kept things clean, spun, wove and dyed the cloth she made, boiled soap, knitted stockings, wove cornhusk mats for the floor, dipped candles, and did a hundred other things.

But busy as they were they had time to be happy.

They were king and queen of their own clearing and John was the prince. Everything they needed they had. When they wanted something they made it. The few things they could not make Caleb got by trading his furs or Jenny's homespuns.

They had done well. In their shed were Lion and Tiger and Bessie the red and white cow. They had a rooster and ten speckled hens, Millie and Whitey the sheep, Diamond the hound, and someday they hoped to have a pig.

One October day their neighbor, Mrs. Hezekiah Lee, invited Jenny to a quilting bee. Jenny took John and was gone all day. At last Caleb grew worried and went down the road to meet her. Not far from the cabin he came upon her. She had John under one arm and a poke under the other, and she was pink with effort and laughter.

"I don't know which wiggles most," said Jenny. "Now, what do you think I have in my poke?"

Caleb couldn't guess, so Jenny gave him John to carry and when they got home she emptied out on the floor of the cabin a little fat pig with a black spot on one side and little black hoofs.

"Mrs. Lee gave him to me," she cried. "Their sow had a bigger litter than she could manage. Isn't he a wonderful little pig?"

"He is wonderful," said Caleb. "I'll build him a little pen tomorrow so the bears won't get him. It will certainly be nice to have our own ham and bacon next fall."

Jenny looked at the little pig as though she didn't like the thought that he would ever be ham and bacon.

A few weeks later she said, "Caleb, do come out and see what John and I have taught the little pig to do."

When Jenny came near the pigsty she raised the pail in which she had the slops and began whistling "Yankee Doodle."

Then the little pig got up on his black hind hoofs and danced in time to the whistle.

"I'm teaching him to turn as he dances," said Jenny. "He's the little pig who danced a jig, isn't he, John?"

Caleb and Jenny laughed at the sight and John laughed because they did.

"A pig that can dance should have a name," said Caleb. "Shall we call him Dancing Tom?"

It was not very long after this that a traveler on horseback stopped at the cabin of Caleb and Jenny to spend the night. He was just back from the newly opened lands along the Mississippi, and had wonderful tales to tell of the richness of the country. As soon as he could make arrangements for taking his family, he would go back.

For many days after the stranger's visit Caleb was more silent than usual, thinking of what the man had told them. At last he said one day:

"Jenny, the land here is not so very good after all. If we went farther west it would be better. Would it be all right for you and John?"

Jenny kissed him.

"John and I want to be wherever you want to be," she said.

Next spring, sometimes alone, sometimes with the help of a neighbor, Caleb began building a flat boat. It was broad and strong. Inside could be carried all they had in their cabin and barn. At the forward end of the deck he built a shed for Lion and Tiger, Bessie, the sheep, and Dancing Tom. At the stern, near the steering sweep, he built a smaller house for Jenny and John and himself. Bessie the cow, not liking the new experience, bawled from the shed, and Jenny whistled "Yankee Doodle" to her pig.

The flat boat started its long journey with Dancing Tom doing a little jig on its deck.

Down the river the flat boat traveled for more than a month.

On fine days Jenny brought her spinning wheel out on deck and worked. John had a rope around his waist to keep him from falling overboard. All the animals soon grew used to floating down the river, and every evening Tom danced for his supper.

"It seems a pity he's ever got to be bacon and ham," sighed Jenny.

One day as they were nearing a turn in the river someone shot arrows at them from the woods. Jenny snatched up John and ran to shelter. The three men poled with all their might, forcing the heavy boat away from the shore. Then Jenny, who had been loading the gun, shot through the windows of the after-house toward the woods. They saw no one. When they were well beyond the bend they counted five arrows in the deck, but no one had been hurt.

Another time they were caught on a sand bar, and it was not until another boat came along and helped them that they were able to get off.

Still another time they hit so hard on a log hidden under the water that it injured the heavy planking and they had to pull ashore for repairs.

In rainy weather it was dull for the animals and dull for Jenny and John in the little after-house. But on sunny days it was gay on deck. There were so many new things to see. There were forests, with here and there a clearing; and boats of all kinds passing quickly down the river and slowly, slowly up the river. Sometimes when they tied up near the shore friendly Indians would come to trade with them.

They always very much admired Dancing Tom.

One night an Indian tried to steal Tom, but Diamond heard him and set up such a terrible barking that the Indian ran away.

Whenever he could, Caleb spent the night near where some other flat boat was moored. Then both families felt safe to go ashore and light a fire and talk until the moon was low in the sky.

Sometimes five or six boats would all be moored close together. Someone was sure to bring out a fiddle and then everyone danced. John, safe in some new friend's lap, would watch Caleb and Jenny dancing with the others. There was no one who could dance them down.

Then sometimes Jenny would show how Tom could dance too. He was more than half grown now, and seemed to enjoy the laughter and hand clapping that greeted his little jig. The fame of Dancing Tom went up and down the river. It seemed a shame that such a clever pig must some day be bacon and ham.

Jenny often talked to Diamond but more often to Tom.

"When we build our new home I'm going to burn that Wandering Foot quilt, which Aunt Sarah gave us when we were married. She called it the Turkey Foot pattern, but I know its real name. Anyone who sleeps under a Wandering Foot quilt has to keep on moving. I like coming down the river but this is far enough. I want John to grow up settled."

Diamond and Dancing Tom always listened carefully to Jenny — especially Dancing Tom.

One day a boat passed them which was painted in bright colors and had its name on the prow and stern — *The Emporium*. It was a store boat, and when Caleb blew on his cow horn it tied up, and he traded for some gingham for Jenny, a new ax-head for himself, and a monkey on a stick for John. Next morning Caleb brought out another surprise for Jenny, a little mirror, so she wouldn't have to do her hair looking down in the pail of water any more.

Where the Ohio joined the Mississippi there was a village of boats. There were house boats and store boats, saloon boats and even a theater boat — all joined together like chips of wood in an eddy. Roosters crowed from the decks, dogs barked, and here and there a cat washed her paws on the roof of a cabin.

There was even a boat where the children went to school. The fame of Dancing Tom had gone before them down the river. School was closed and all the children ran out on deck with their teacher to watch Tom dance when the Fosters' boat tied up near them.

"Hurrah! hurrah! for Dancing Tom!" they shouted.

Caleb did not stay long in the village of boats — just long enough to ask some questions about land. He decided to go downriver. If he had gone upriver he would have had to hire many boatmen, to pole and haul and drag his boat against the wide yellow waters of the Mississippi. Even going down the river was dangerous. He learned all he could about the bad stretches, and then started out as boldly as ever.

After only a week on the twisting waters of the great river Caleb found land that he liked the looks of. There was a spring on it, and some of the land was open and some was wooded. He and his companions moored the flat boat for the last time and the next day began to take it apart.

First they built, on shore, a cabin of its timbers. Caleb had even brought brick with him for a chimney.

Then they built a barn for Lion and Tiger, Bessie, the two sheep and Dancing Tom. For a while the animals lived in very unsheltered quarters on the half-torn-down flat boat, but soon they, too, were ashore with good earth under their hoofs.

How the rooster crowed the first morning on their own land!

The leftover timbers they split for the first fence rails and Caleb made a doorstep from the blade of the sweep.

"It has steered us for hundreds of miles," he said, "now it should settle down with us."

Jenny liked the new house. She planted some rose shoots she had brought with her, and hollyhock seeds by the door. Caleb built a fence around her flowers to protect them.

"Tom had better run loose," he said. "There's nothing like a hog for keeping new land clear of snakes."

"Wouldn't a rattler kill him?" asked Jenny. She was very fond of her pig.

"No," said Caleb. "Somehow the poison doesn't go through their fat. Hogs like to eat rattlesnakes about as much as acorns."

So daytimes Dancing Tom ran loose, though still Jenny whistled "Yankee Doodle" for him when she brought out the slops, and still he rose up to his hind feet and danced for her. John was getting big enough to enjoy the game. He would dance too, imitating Tom.

It was a sight that made Jenny laugh and laugh even after the hardest day's work. Caleb laughed too, but he said:

"Tom's growing into a regular hog. Soon it will be time to turn him into bacon and ham."

Then Jenny looked sad.

The weeks went by. The men who had come down the river with them went away on their own adventures. Jenny secretly burned the Wandering Foot quilt. She wanted to stay here always with the huge river at her feet. At first she was afraid that John might fall into it, but soon she could trust him to keep away from the bank. He was a handsome little boy, full of curiosity and courage. Caleb and Jenny thought he was the finest little boy in the world.

One day Jenny was hoeing in the garden near the cabin. It was a day so fine that all the birds were singing. The hens were scratching contentedly in the dust. The cattle and sheep were grazing among the burned-over stumps of the clearing. By the shed, wandering where he wanted to, was Dancing Tom.

Little John was near her, very earnestly digging a hole in the dirt with an old spoon.

Caleb and Diamond had gone hunting, but Jenny liked to be alone. She was not afraid, and she was not lonely. Only when she looked at Tom she felt sad. She couldn't keep him much longer, she knew.

Just then she noticed that Millie, the black-nosed sheep, seemed to have caught her foot in a hole.

"I don't want her to break a leg," thought Jenny, as she climbed over the fence. She had to go toward Millie very slowly so as not to frighten her and make her jerk her leg.

"Here, Millie, nice Millie," she called, holding out her hand as though there were salt in it.

Millie stared with her gray agate eyes and breathed hard, but at last she let Jenny get near her. The poor leg had been caught between two stones, but Jenny pulled it free safely.

"Mind where you're going, Millie," she said.

She turned back toward her garden. Everything looked so

nice from here, the river seen through the trees, and the cabin with unbroken glass in every window. There was John, bless him, not far from where she had left him, and after something as usual. She'd find a ladybug or butterfly in his fat little hand.

It was not until Jenny was climbing the fence again that she knew what John was after. She heard before she saw, heard that rattling like dry peas quickly shaken in a dipper, and then she saw the flat arrow-shaped head above the coils of the rattlesnake.

Jenny was used to acting quickly, but no woman could have reached the snake before John did. As she ran, she called out; but John was too interested to hear her. She saw him take another step and reach out his hand.

Jenny kept on running and calling.

But it was Tom that reached the snake first, grunting with satisfaction. The flat head struck twice at the hog, but then Tom's hoofs came down on its back and broke it. Jenny snatched up John.

"Naughty Tom! Naughty Tom!" screamed John, beating on Jenny's shoulder with his fists. He howled with rage. He had wanted that thing which rattled and Tom had taken it away from him. Jenny cried too, but she cried from joy.

When Caleb and Diamond came home that evening Jenny ran to meet them, holding John tight by the hand.

"I have so much to tell you," she cried. "I don't know where to begin!"

Caleb hung up a fine turkey under the eaves.

"Let's begin with supper then, Jenny," he said. "A hungry man has no ears. After supper, we'll sit on the doorstep and I'll light my pipe to keep away the mosquitoes, and then you can tell me."

Jenny could scarcely bear to keep silence that long, but she managed to serve the venison stew and the corn pones she had cooked in the ashes, the buttermilk and the stirabout pudding.

At last the meal was over and they were sitting side by side on the doorsill of the cabin, their feet upon the sweep blade of the flat boat. Caleb filled his pipe and Jenny ran to get him a coal from the fire in the small tongs, stopping a moment to take another look at John in his cradle by the hearth. Caleb lighted his pipe.

"Now tell me," he said.

When Jenny had told him the story of Millie, and John and the rattlesnake and Tom, Caleb drew a long breath.

"Look, I've saved the rattles," said Jenny.

Caleb counted them. There were eleven.

"A big snake," said Caleb. "Still, even a little one would have been big enough to kill John."

First Caleb went in to see John in his cradle by the hearth. The little boy seemed so full of courage and curiosity, even in his sleep. Caleb stood a long time looking down at his son and Jenny stood beside him, saying nothing.

Then Caleb went out to where Tom was still rooting and grunting in the last of the sunlight. Caleb watched him for quite a while too.

"From now on," he said suddenly, "your name's Dancing Tom Foster."

Dancing Tom paid no attention, but Jenny said quickly, with shining eyes:

"Then he doesn't have to be ham and bacon — ever?"

"Certainly not," said Caleb. "Didn't you hear me say that his name was Foster? From now on he's one of the family."

Then Jenny laughed, and hearing her laugh Caleb laughed too; and at so much laughter Dancing Tom grunted absent-mindedly, and getting to his short hind legs danced a rather short jig, for he was growing stout and easily got out of breath.

Death of Red Peril

Walter D. Edmonds

John brought his off eye to bear on me: —

What do them old coots down to the store do? Why, one of 'em will think up a horse that's been dead forty year and then they'll set around remembering this and that about that horse until they've made a resurrection of him. You'd think he was a regular Grattan Bars, the way they talk, telling one thing and another, when a man knows if that horse hadn't 've had a breeching to keep his tail end off the ground he could hardly have walked from here to Boonville.

A horse race is a handsome thing to watch if a man has his money on a sure proposition. My pa was always a great hand at a horse race. But when he took to a boat and my mother he didn't have no more time for it. So he got interested in another sport.

Did you ever hear of racing caterpillars? No? Well, it used to be a great thing on the canawl. My pa used to have a lot of them insects on hand every fall, and the way he could get them to run would make a man have his eyes examined.

The way we raced caterpillars was to set them in a napkin

18

ring on a table, one facing one way and one the other. Outside the napkin ring was drawed a circle in chalk three feet acrost. Then a man lifted the ring and the handlers was allowed one jab with a darning needle to get their caterpillars started. The one that got outside the chalk circle the first was the one that won the race.

I remember my pa tried out a lot of breeds, and he got hold of some pretty fast steppers. But there wasn't one of them could equal Red Peril. To see him you wouldn't believe he could run. He was all red and kind of stubby, and he had a sort of wart behind that you'd think would get in his way. There wasn't anything fancy in his looks. He'd just set still studying the ground and make you think he was dreaming about last year's oats; but when you set him in the starting ring he'd hitch himself up behind like a man lifting on his galluses, and then he'd light out for glory.

Pa come acrost Red Peril down in Westernville. Ma's relatives resided there, and it being Sunday we'd all gone in to church. We was riding back in a hired rig with a dandy trotter, and Pa was pushing her right along and Ma was talking sermon and clothes, and me and my sister was setting on the back seat playing poke your nose, when all of a sudden Pa hollers, "Whoa!" and set the horse right down on the breeching. Ma let out a holler and come to rest on the dashboard with her head under the horse. "My gracious land!" she says. "What's happened?" Pa was out on the other side of the road right down in the mud in his Sunday pants, a-wropping up something in his yeller handkerchief. Ma begun to get riled. "What you doing, Pa?" she says. "What you got there?" Pa was putting his handkerchief back into his inside pocket.

Then he come back over the wheel and got him a chew. "Leeza," he says, "I got the fastest caterpillar in seven counties. It's an act of Providence I seen him, the way he jumped the ruts." "It's an act of God I ain't laying dead under the back end of that horse," says Ma. "I've gone and spoilt my Sunday hat." "Never mind," says Pa; "Red Peril will earn you a new one." Just like that he named him. He was the fastest caterpillar in seven counties.

When we got back onto the boat, while Ma was turning up the supper, Pa set him down to the table under the lamp and pulled out the handkerchief. "You two devils stand there and there," he says to me and my sister, "and if you let him get by I'll leather the soap out of you."

So we stood there and he undid the handkerchief, and out walked one of them red, long-haired caterpillars. He walked right to the middle of the table, and then he took a short turn and put his nose in his tail and went to sleep.

"Who'd think that insect could make such a break for freedom as I seen him make?" says Pa, and he got out a empty Brandreth box and filled it up with some towel and put the caterpillar inside. "He needs a rest," says Pa. "He needs to get used to his stall. When he limbers up I'll commence training him. Now then," he says, putting the box on the shelf back of the stove, "don't none of you say a word about him."

He got out a pipe and set there smoking and figuring, and we could see he was studying out just how he'd make a world-beater out of that bug. "What you going to feed him?" asks Ma. "If I wasn't afraid of constipating him," Pa says, "I'd try him out with milkweed."

Next day we hauled up the Lansing Kill Gorge. Ned

Kilbourne, Pa's driver, come aboard in the morning, and he took a look at that caterpillar. He took him out of the box and felt his legs and laid him down on the table and went clean over him. "Well," he says, "he don't look like a great lot, but I've knowed some of that red variety could chug along pretty smart." Then he touched him with a pin. It was a sudden sight.

It looked like the rear end of that caterpillar was racing the front end, but it couldn't never quite get by. Afore either Ned or Pa could get a move Red Peril had made a turn around the sugar bowl and run solid aground in the butter dish.

Pa let out a loud swear. "Look out he don't pull a tendon," he says. "Butter's a bad thing. A man has to be careful. Jeepers," he says, picking him up and taking him over to the stove to dry, "I'll handle him myself. I don't want no rum-soaked bezabors dishing my beans."

"I didn't mean harm, Will," says Ned. "I was just curious."

There was something extraordinary about that caterpillar. He was intelligent. It seemed he just couldn't abide the feel of sharp iron. It got so that if Pa reached for the lapel of his coat Red Peril would light out. It must have been he was tender. I said he had a sort of wart behind, and I guess he liked to find it a place of safety.

We was all terrible proud of that bird. Pa took to timing him on the track. He beat all known time holler. He got to know that as soon as he crossed the chalk he would get back safe in his quarters. Only when we tried sprinting him across the supper table, if he saw a piece of butter he'd pull up short and bolt back where he come from. He had a mortal fear of butter.

21

Well, Pa trained him three nights. It was a sight to see him there at the table, a big man with a needle in his hand, moving the lamp around and studying out the identical spot that caterpillar wanted most to get out of the needle's way. Pretty soon he found it, and then he says to Ned, "I'll race him agin all comers at all odds." "Well, Will," says Ned, "I guess it's a safe proposition."

We hauled up the feeder to Forestport and got us a load of potatoes. We raced him there against Charley Mack, the bankwalker's, Leopard Pillar, one of them tufted breeds with a row of black buttons down the back. The Leopard was well liked and had won several races that season, and there was quite a few boaters around that fancied him. Pa argued for favorable odds, saying he was racing a maiden caterpillar; and there was a lot of money laid out, and Pa and Ned managed to cover the most of it. As for the race, there wasn't anything to it. While we was putting him in the ring — one of them birchbark and sweet grass ones Indians make — Red Peril didn't act very good. I guess the smell and the crowd kind of upset him. He was nervous and kept fidgeting with his front feet; but they hadn't more 'n lifted the ring than he lit out under the edge as tight as he could make it, and Pa touched him with the needle just as he lepped the line. My and my sister was supposed to be in bed, but Ma had gone visiting in Forestport and we'd snuck in and was under the table, which had a red cloth onto it, and I can tell you there was some shouting. There was some couldn't believe that insect had been inside the ring at all; and there was some said he must be a cross with a dragon fly or a side-hill gouger; but old Charley Mack, that'd worked in the camps, said he guessed Red Peril must be descended from the caterpillars Paul Bunyan used to race. He said you could tell by the bump on his tail, which Paul used to put on all his caterpillars, seeing as how the smallest pointed object he could hold in his hand was a peavy.

Well, Pa raced him a couple of more times and he won just as easy, and Pa cleared up close to a hundred dollars in three races. That caterpillar was a mammoth wonder, and word of him got going and people commenced talking him up everywhere, so it was hard to race him around these parts.

But about that time the dock-keeper of Number One on the feeder come across a pretty swift article that the people round Rome thought high of. And as our boat was headed down the gorge, word got ahead about Red Peril, and people began to look out for the race.

We come into Number One about four o'clock, and Pa tied up right there and went on shore with his box in his pocket and Red Peril inside the box. There must have been ten men crowded into the shanty, and as many more again outside looking in the windows and door. The lock-tender was a skinny bezabor from Stittville, who thought he knew a lot about racing caterpillars; and, come to think of it, maybe he did. His name was Henry Buscerck, and he had a bad tooth in front he used to suck at a lot.

Well, him and Pa set their caterpillars on the table for the crowd to see, and I must say Buscerck's caterpillar was as handsome a brute as you could wish to look at, bright bay with black points and a short fine coat. He had a way of looking right and left, too, that made him handsome. But Pa didn't bother to look at him. Red Peril was a natural marvel, and he knew it.

Buscerck was a sly, twerpish man, and he must 've heard about Red Peril — right from the beginning, as it turned out; for he laid out the course in yeller chalk. They used Pa's ring, a big silver one he'd bought secondhand just for Red Peril. They laid out a lot of money, and Dennison Smith lifted the ring. The way Red Peril histed himself out from under would raise a man's blood pressure twenty notches. I swear you could see the hair lay down on his back. Why, that black-pointed bay was left nowhere! It didn't seem like he moved. But Red Peril was just gathering himself for a fast finish over the line when he seen it was yeller. He reared right up; he must 've thought it was butter, by Jeepers, the way he whirled on his hind legs and went the way he'd come. Pa begun to get scared, and he shook his needle behind Red Peril, but that caterpillar was more scared of butter than he ever was of cold steel. He passed the other insect afore he'd got halfway to the line. By Cripus, you'd ought to 've heard the cheering from the Forestport crews. The Rome men was green. But when he got to the line, danged if that caterpillar didn't shy again and run around the circle twicet, and then it seemed like his heart had gone in on him, and he crept right back to the middle of the circle and lay there hiding his head. It was the pitifulest sight a man ever looked at. You could almost hear him moaning, and he shook all over.

I've never seen a man so riled as Pa was. The water was running right out of his eyes. He picked up Red Peril and he says, "This here's no race." He picked up his money and he says, "The course was illegal, with that yeller chalk." Then he squashed the other caterpillar, which was just getting ready to cross the line, and he looks at Buscerck and says, "What 're you going to do about that?"

Buscerck says, "I'm going to collect my money. My cater-pillar would have beat."

"If you want to call that a finish you can," says Pa, point-ing to the squashed bay one, "but a baby could see he's still got to reach the line. Red Peril got to wire and come back and got to it again afore your hayseed worm got half his feet on the ground. If it was any other man owned him," Pa says, "I'd feel sorry I squashed him."

He stepped out of the house, but Buscerck laid a-hold of his pants and says, "You got to pay, Hemstreet. A man can't get away with no such excuses in the city of Rome."

Pa didn't say nothing. He just hauled off and sunk his fist, and Buscerck come to inside the lock, which was at low level right then. He waded out the lower end and he says, "I'll have you arrested for this." Pa says, "All right; but if I ever catch you around this lock again I'll let you have a feel with your other eye."

Nobody else wanted to collect money from Pa, on account of his build, mostly, so we went back to the boat. Pa put Red Peril to bed for two days. It took him all of that to get over his fright at the yeller circle. Pa even made us go without butter for a spell, thinking Red Peril might know the smell of it. He was such an intelligent, thinking animal, a man couldn't tell nothing about him.

But next morning the sheriff comes aboard and arrests Pa with a warrant and takes him afore a justice of the peace. That was old Oscar Snipe. He'd heard all about the race, and I think he was feeling pleasant with Pa, because right off they commenced talking breeds. It would have gone off good only

Pa'd been having a round with the sheriff. They come in arm in arm, singing a Hallelujah meeting song; but Pa was polite, and when Oscar says, "What's this?" he only says, "Well, well."

"I hear you've got a good caterpillar," says the judge.

"Well, well," says Pa. It was all he could think of to say.

"What breed is he?" says Oscar, taking a chew.

"Well," says Pa, "well, well."

Ned Kilbourne says he was a red one.

"That's a good breed," says Oscar, folding his hands on his stummick and spitting over his thumbs and between his knees and into the sandbox all in one spit. "I kind of fancy the yeller ones myself. You're a connesewer," he says to Pa, "and so 'm I, and between connesewers I'd like to show you one. He's as neat a stepper as there is in this county."

"Well, well," says Pa, kind of cold around the eyes and looking at the lithograph of Mrs. Snipe done in a hair frame over the sink.

Oscar slews around and fetches a box out of his back pocket and shows us a sweet little yeller one.

"There she is," he says, and waits for praise.

"She was a good woman," Pa said after a while, looking at the picture, "if any woman that's four times a widow can be called such."

"Not her," says Oscar. "It's this yeller caterpillar."

Pa slung his eyes on the insect which Oscar was holding, and it seemed like he'd just got an idee.

"Fast?" he says, deep down. "That thing run! Why, a snail with the stringhalt could spit in his eye."

Old Oscar come to a boil quick.

"Evidence. Bring me the evidence."

He spit, and he was that mad he let his whole chew get away from him without noticing. Buscerck says, "Here," and takes his hand off 'n his right eye.

Pa never took no notice of nothing after that but the eye. It was the shiniest black onion I ever see on a man. Oscar says, "Forty dollars!" And Pa pays and says, "It's worth it."

But it don't never pay to make an enemy in horse racing or caterpillars, as you will see, after I've got around to telling you.

Well, we raced Red Peril nine times after that, all along the Big Ditch, and you can hear to this day — yes, sir — that there never was a caterpillar alive could run like Red Peril. Pa got rich onto him. He allowed to buy a new team in the spring. If he could only 've started a breed from that bug, his fortune would 've been made and Henry Ford would've looked like a bent nickel alongside me to-day. But caterpillars aren't built like Ford cars. We beat all the great caterpillars of the year, and it being a time for a late winter, there was some fast running. We raced the Buffalo Big Blue and Fenwick's Night Mail and Wilson's Joe of Barneveld. There wasn't one could touch Red Peril. It was close into October when a crowd got together and brought up the Black Arrer of Ava to race us, but Red Peril beat him by an inch. And after that there wasn't a caterpillar in the state would race Pa's.

He was mighty chesty them days and had come to be quite a figger down the canawl. People come aboard to talk with him and admire Red Peril; and Pa got the idea of charging five cents a sight, and that made for more money even if there wasn't no more running for the animile. He commenced to get fat.

And then come the time that comes to all caterpillars. And it goes to show that a man ought to be as careful of his enemies as he is lending money to friends.

We was hauling down the Lansing Kill again and we'd just crossed the aqueduct over Stringer Brook when the lock-keep-er, that minded it and the lock just below, come out and says there was quite a lot of money being put up on a caterpillar they'd collected down in Rome.

Well, Pa went in and he got out Red Peril and tried him out. He was fat and his stifles acted kind of stiff, but you could see with half an eye he was still fast. His start was a mite slower, but he made great speed once he got going.

"He's not in the best shape in the world," Pa says, "and if it was any other bug I wouldn't want to run him. But I'll trust the old brute," and he commenced brushing him up with a toothbrush he'd bought a-purpose.

"Yeanh," says Ned. "It may not be right, but we've got to consider the public."

By what happened after, we might have known that we'd meet up with that caterpillar at Number One Lock; but there wasn't no sign of Buscerck, and Pa was so excited at racing Red Peril again that I doubt if he noticed where he was at all. He was all rigged out for the occasion. He had on a black hat and a new red boating waistcoat, and when he busted loose with his horn for the lock you'd have thought he wanted to wake up all the deef-and-dumbers in seven counties. We tied by the upper gates and left the team to graze; and there was quite a crowd on hand. About nine morning boats was tied along the tow-path, and all the afternoon boats waited. People was hanging around, and when they heard Pa whanging his horn they let out a great cheer. He took off his hat to some of the ladies, and then he took Red Peril out of his pocket and everybody cheered some more.

"Who owns this-here caterpillar I've been hearing about?" Pa asks. "Where is he? Why don't he bring out his pore contraption?"

A feller says he's in the shanty.

"What's his name?" says Pa.

"Martin Henry's running him. He's called the Horned Demon of Rome."

"Dinged if I ever thought to see him at my time of life," says Pa. And he goes in. Inside there was a lot of men talking and smoking and drinking and laying money faster than Leghorns can lay eggs, and when Pa comes in they let out a great howdy, and when Pa put down the Brandreth box on the table they crowded round; and you'd ought to 've heard the mammoth shout they give when Red Peril climbed out of his box. And well they might. Yes, sir!

You can tell that caterpillar's a thoroughbred. He's shining right down to the root of each hair. He's round, but he ain't too fat. He don't look as supple as he used to, but the folks can't tell that. He's got the winner's look, and he prances into the centre of the ring with a kind of delicate canter that was as near single-footing as I ever see a caterpillar get to. By Jeepers Cripus! I felt proud to be in the same family as him, and I wasn't only a little lad.

Pa waits for the admiration to die down, and he lays out his money, and he says to Martin Henry, "Let's see your ring-boned swivel-hocked imitation of a bug."

Martin answers, "Well, he ain't much to look at, maybe, but you'll be surprised to see how he can push along."

And he lays down the dangedest lump of worm you ever set your eyes on. It's the kind of insect a man might expect to see in France or one of them furrin lands. It's about two and a half inches long and stands only half a thumbnail at the shoulder. It's green and as hairless as a newborn egg, and it crouches down squinting around at Red Peril like a man with sweat in his eye. It ain't natural nor refined to look at such a bug, let alone race it.

When Pa seen it, he let out a shout and laughed. He couldn't talk from laughing.

But the crowd didn't say a lot, having more money on the race than ever was before or since on a similar occasion. It was so much that even Pa commenced to be serious. Well, they put 'em in the ring together and Red Peril kept over on his side with a sort of intelligent dislike. He was the brainiest article in the caterpillar line I ever knowed. The other one just hunkered down with a mean look in his eye.

Millard Thompson held the ring. He counted, "One — two — three — and off." Some folks said it was the highest he knew how to count, but he always got that far anyhow, even if it took quite a while for him to remember what figger to commence with.

The ring come off and Pa and Martin Henry sunk their needles — at least they almost sunk them, for just then them standing close to the course seen that Horned Demon sink his horns into the back end of Red Peril. He was always a sensitive animal, Red Peril was, and if a needle made him start you can think for yourself what them two horns did for him. He cleared twelve inches in one jump — but then he sot right down on his belly, trembling.

"Foul!" bellers Pa. "My 'pillar's fouled."

"It ain't in the rule book," Millard says.

"It's a foul!" yells Pa; and all the Forestport men yell, "Foul! Foul!"

But it wasn't allowed. The Horned Demon commenced walking to the circle — he couldn't move much faster than a barrel can roll uphill, but he was getting there. We all seen two things, then. Red Peril was dying, and we was losing the race. Pa stood there kind of foamy in his beard, and the water running right out of both eyes. It's an awful thing to see a big man cry in public. But Ned saved us. He seen Red Peril was dying, the way he wiggled, and he figgered, with the money he had on him, he'd make him win if he could.

He leans over and puts his nose into Red Peril's ear, and he shouts, "My Cripus, you've gone and dropped the butter!"

Something got into that caterpillar's brain, dying as he was, and he let out the smallest squeak of a hollering fright I ever listened to a caterpillar make. There was a convulsion got into him. He looked like a three-dollar mule with the wind colic, and then he gave a bound. My holy! How that caterpillar did rise up. When he come down again, he was stone dead, but he lay with his chin across the line. He'd won the race. The Horned Demon was blowing bad and only halfway to the line . . . .

Well, we won. But I think Pa's heart was busted by the squeal he heard Red Peril make when he died. He couldn't

31

abide Ned's face after that, though he knowed Ned had saved the day for him. But he put Red Peril's carcase in his pocket with the money and walks out.

And there he seen Buscerck standing at the sluices. Pa stood looking at him. The sheriff was alongside Buscerck and Oscar Snipe on the other side, and Buscerck guessed he had the law behind him.

"Who owns that Horned Demon?" said Pa.

"Me," says Buscerck with a sneer. "He may have lost, but he done a good job doing it."

Pa walks right up to him.

"I've got another forty dollars in my pocket," he says, and he connected sizeably.

Buscerck's boots showed a minute. Pretty soon they let down the water and pulled him out. They had to roll a couple of gallons out of him afore they got a grunt. It served him right. He'd played foul. But the sheriff was worried, and he says to Oscar, "Had I ought to arrest Will?" (Meaning Pa.)

Oscar was a sporting man. He couldn't abide low dealing. He looks at Buscerck there, shaping his belly over the barrel, and he says, "Water never hurt a man. It keeps his hide from cracking." So they let Pa alone. I guess they didn't think it was safe to have a man in jail that would cry about a caterpillar. But then they hadn't lived alongside of Red Peril like us.

Down from the Hills
From the Hills of Tennessee, to Arkansas and Back

Lois Lenski

"Where we goin', Ma?"

A little girl sat on top of the wagon. It was piled high with bedding, bundles, and boxes.

"We're goin' to Arkansas to pick cotton," said her mother.

"Is *this* Arkansas, Ma?" asked the girl.

"Yes, but there's no cotton here," said Ma. "We got to go farther south. Is that wheel near-about fixed, Big Joe?"

Trixie's big brother was kneeling on the ground. He pounded boards on a wobbly wheel of the second wagon.

"Yes, *ma'm*," said the boy. "I got her fixed. Let's go, Pa."

He spoke to a man who came out from the yard of a nearby house, followed by a younger boy. They brought water in buckets, which they poured into a milk-can. Big Joe put the cover on tight and lifted the can up.

"Let's go!" said the man, climbing on the first wagon and taking the reins.

Pa Medley was a lanky, unshaven man dressed in overalls. He whistled sharply and three hound dogs came running. Little Jeff jumped on the rear end, leading a small pony by a rope.

Big Joe took his place beside Old Granny and drove the second wagon. Trixie and her mother dangled their bare legs over the side. The wagons began to move, with the dogs trotting underneath.

"I was a-scared on that ferry," said Trixie. "River so big and wide and all. I was a-scared we'd fall in."

"Biggest, widest river in the world — the Mississippi," said Big Joe. "Never seen it so low before. We coulda waded over."

"Waded over and got drownded," said Trixie.

"Can't git from Tennessee to Arkansas without crossin' that big ole river," said Ma. She took a pinch of snuff from the can in her pocket and tucked it inside her lower lip.

"I wisht I was back home again, back in the hills where we come from," said Trixie sadly. "Don't like no river, don't like Arkansas, don't like cotton-pickin'."

"You hush up, Trixie," said Ma. "You can pick cotton jest like the rest of us. You not a baby no more."

"I ain't homesick, Ma," called Little Jeff. "I'll pick cotton for you."

The little caravan moved slowly on. Cars and trucks passed it by. People put out their heads and looked. People in houses along the road came out and stared. Old Granny shook out her pipe and began to sing *Rock of Ages* in a quavering voice.

"Why's all the folks lookin' at us?" asked Trixie.

"They ain't never seen a hoss before, I reckon," laughed Big Joe. "Hosses gone clean outa style over here in Arkansas."

The rolling hills flattened out and the cotton fields looked larger. Some were filled with pickers. But there were no signs saying: *Pickers Needed.* Pa Medley stopped his horses and hailed a man walking.

"Know where there's any cotton to pick?" he asked.

"No, I don't," said the man, staring.

They kept on going. They did not know whom to ask about cotton-picking jobs. They felt like strangers in a strange land. It was near nightfall when they pulled up at a corner. A small country church stood across the road opposite a country store. A few houses were just beyond.

"Oh, look at the purty little church-house," said Ma.

"And there's a store," said Pa. "See all them cotton-pickers goin' in. There's bound to be plenty cotton to pick around here."

"Not much grass for the hosses," said Big Joe.

"All the fields are growed to cotton," said Pa. "Plumb out to the road."

"That grass in the churchyard looks good," said Ma.

"Sure does," said Pa. "Best we've seen since we left the hills."

"We'll camp in the churchyard," said Ma. "A church-house belongs to everybody. Nobody'll bother us there."

"Good!" said Granny. "Let's sleep in the churchyard."

They drove slowly in. They stopped at the back, as far from the road as possible. Trixie and Little Jeff jumped down to stretch their legs. The youngest hound-puppy scampered about with them. Trixie ran to the door of the church-house and opened it a crack. She and Little Jeff peeked in. Ma came up behind them.

"See! The door's open," she said. "They keep it open so people can come in and rest — and say their prayers." She looked inside. "It sure is purty. So nice and clean. Such purty cushions on them benches — the color o' wild roses."

"We gonna sleep in the church-house?" asked Trixie.

35

"We could each have a bench to ourself," said Little Jeff.

Ma closed the door quickly. "No, we ain't," she said. "It'll be a sight cooler sleepin' outdoors." They walked back to the wagon. "I'd sure like to come to meetin' here jest once, to hear the preachin' and singin'." She began to unpack and get ready for supper.

"Trixie," called Ma, handing her a quarter. "Go over to that store and buy us a quarter's worth o' coffee."

"Ask if anybody needs cotton pickers," said Pa.

"Ask if it's all right for us to sleep in the churchyard," said Ma.

"I'm a-scared to go," said the little girl.

"Go on, nothin' ain't gonna bite you, honey."

The little girl ran across the road.

Trixie slipped into the store and looked around.

A truckload of Mexican cotton-pickers came up and stopped. Men, women, and children crowded into the store. They made gestures and talked loudly in a strange language. They pointed to bologna, crackers, bread, and canned goods. The storekeepers filled up many paper bags with groceries.

Trixie was hemmed in. She stared through the dirty glass of the candy case at the back. She kept her eyes fixed on the candy. After the cotton-pickers went out, a boy came in.

"Hi, George!" called the storekeeper.

"Hi, Jim!" said George. "There's a bunch of gypsies campin' in the churchyard. Betcha they're gonna steal things tonight. Better lock your store up tight."

The storekeeper laughed. "I seen 'em come a while ago, but I don't guess they're thieves. They couldn't git away fast enough in them rickety ole wagons. Thieves have cars nowadays."

"Horse-thieves, maybe," said George. "They got so many horses. Or maybe they're horse-traders."

"How do you get such big ideas, boy?" asked Jim Harter.

"I bet they stole that bicycle they got up on that front wagon," said George.

"Likely they're jest country folks goin' on a journey to visit their kinfolk," said Jim.

George looked back and saw the little girl by the candy case. He pointed with his thumb. "There's one of 'em, Jim," he said. "Better watch her. She'll snitch a cracker or somethin'."

"I'm not worried," said Jim.

The boy went out and a well-dressed man came in. He had parked his large black car out front.

"Howdy, Mr. Bryce," nodded Jim Harter. "What can I do for you?"

"My son Edward came home from school today," said the man, "and reported that gypsies were camping in the churchyard. So I came right over."

"There they are." Jim pointed out the window. "Take a look."

"Where are they from?" asked Mr. Bryce. "What do they want?"

"Dunno, Mr. Bryce," said Jim. "I ain't asked 'em. It ain't none of my business."

"Well, as President of the Board of Trustees of the Promised Land Church," said Mr. Bryce, "I think it *is my* business . . ."

Mrs. Bryce hurried in.

"I went over close and looked, Randolph," she said in an agitated tone. "They're terrible people. The Ladies' Aid

37

has just put those new rose-colored cushions on the pews. If they go in, they'll sleep on them sure, and likely they've all got . . . you-know-what. They're not clean, anybody can see that. They're all in their bare feet. It took six pie-suppers to buy that upholstery cloth. We paid $4.98 a yard for it."

Several other cars drove up and people hurried in. "You seen 'em?" The heads nodded, and a confusion of talk filled the store.

"They'll go right in and sleep soon as it's dark," said Mrs. Bryce. "The door's unlocked, you know."

"Remember the time those picnickers got in and tore up all the hymn-books?" asked Mrs. Hollis.

"Why do you leave the door unlocked then?" Jim Harter, who never went to church, sounded angry.

"Well . . ." Mrs. Bryce began, "it's the House of God . . . and it's kept open for prayer and meditation."

"Let 'em go in!" said Jim Harter. "They need to pray and meditate." A smile passed over his angry face.

Mr. Bryce had been talking to the men. "We'll be legal about this," he said. "We'll call the State Police." He went to the telephone behind the counter and had a short conversation. Then he told the crowd, "They'll be right out. They'll take care of it."

"Well, I'll be dog-goned!" exclaimed Jim Harter.

The store was quiet after the people left. It was dark too, so Jim turned on a light. Then he saw that the little girl was still there. He went back to her.

"What you want, sister?" he asked softly.

Trixie put the quarter in his hand and whispered the word

coffee. The man poured some ground coffee in a paper sack and handed it to her. "Anything else?" he asked.

The girl kept on staring into the candy case. Quickly Jim Harter reached in and picked up a stick of candy. "Here!" he said, handing it out. "Here's some candy for you."

The man's kind words had the effect of the shot of a gun on a frightened rabbit. One minute the girl was there, the next minute she was gone. Her thin figure like a fleeting shadow leaped across the road. The storekeeper was left standing with the candy in his hand.

"Well, I'll be dog-goned!" he said.

The campfire was burning nicely. The pot of coffee was boiling and its fragrance filled the air. Big Joe chopped more sticks and put them on. There was just enough wind to make the sparks fly. Trixie loved a fire. She squatted down and watched it. Old Granny sat on a box near by singing *Jesus Lover of My Soul.* Trixie went over, leaned against her, and the two sang together. They stopped abruptly when they saw they were not alone.

A crowd of people had come into the churchyard. The boy George was right in front. A buzz of conversation began. Trixie ran to her mother, who was setting out food for supper.

"I'm a-scared, Ma," she cried. "What's all them people come here for? Why can't they go away and leave us alone?"

A State Police car drove up and a man stepped out. After talking to Mr. Bryce, the policeman came over. "I'm sorry," he said to Pa Medley, "but you folks can't camp here."

Medley bristled. "What right you got to order us off? You're not the preacher, be you?"

The policeman opened his coat and showed his badge.

"*Po*-lice, be you?" gasped Medley.

"Oh Ma, it's the *Po*-lice!" cried Trixie. "They takin' us to the jail-house, all for me and Granny singin'? Can't we sing hymns, not even in the churchyard?"

"Hush up," said Ma. "You hush up, Trixie."

Pa Medley never liked to be bossed around by somebody else.

"Well, we'll study about it," he told the policeman.

Ma felt suddenly brave. "We'll go when we git good and ready," she said.

"Oh Ma, don't let 'em take us to the jail-house!" cried Little Jeff. *"We ain't done nothin' bad."*

"No camping allowed in the churchyard," repeated the policeman. "The trustees of the Promised Land Church don't like it. You'd better be moving along."

Suddenly Jim Harter was there. "Hey, officer," he cried. "These folks are all right. They're honest, they won't steal a thing." But no one listened. "They're just goin' to visit their kinfolk," cried Jim. But nobody listened.

When Pa Medley saw that the officer meant what he said, he gave in. "We was jest goin'," he said weakly. "We'll move on like you say."

The policeman went into the church, where he saw that everything was in order. "They haven't hurt a thing," he reported to Mr. Bryce. "Haven't even set a foot inside the door."

Old Granny roused up and exclaimed: "What's this? They won't let us sleep in the churchyard? Why not? Why not?" She began to sing:

40

"Sleepin' in the churchyard,
There I'll rest my head;
Gittin' my eternal rest,
As cosy as in bed . . ."

Pa Medley and the boys began putting mattress, buckets, bicycle, boxes and bundles back on the wagons. Big Joe hitched up the horses.

"They'll move on now," repeated the policeman to Mr. Bryce. "Call me again if they give you any further trouble." He hopped in the police car and drove off.

Mr. Bryce and the others went home. No one was left to watch as the two wagons pulled slowly out of the churchyard. No one but Jim Harter, staring out through his darkened store window.

"What we done, Ma?" asked Trixie, her eyes full of fear.

"Nothin'," said Ma. "They don't want us to sleep there, that's all."

"What did the *Po*-lice come for? To put us in the jail-house?" Little Jeff was crying noisily.

"You better hush up," said Ma, "or that *Po*-lice will hear you and come back and ketch you."

Little Jeff hushed up promptly, a look of terror in his eyes.

The wagons creaked along the road. The setting sun had sunk behind a fringe of trees beyond the cotton fields. Darkness fell.

"Wisht we could find grass for the hosses," said Big Joe.

"They don't use horses here no more," said Pa, "only tractors. Them machines don't eat no grass."

"Grass and trees would make nice shade on a hot summer day," said Ma.

"Shade don't fill their pockets with money like cotton does," said Pa. "Every inch is planted to cotton."

The family spoke sadly in low voices. They were not angry or resentful. They accepted what came. When you are far from home, you never know what to expect. They were strangers in a strange land.

"That boy's name was George," said Trixie. "He was in the store, and he come over to see the *Po*-lice too. He called the storekeeper Jim. He told Jim we was gypsies and thieves. What's *gypsies,* Ma?"

"I dunno," said Ma. "Hush up now, Trixie. You talk too much."

Pa Medley pulled the horses up at the side of the road.

"Might as well stop here," he called back to Big Joe on the second wagon. "It's night already. We got to sleep somewheres."

The paved highway had a bank at one side covered with weeds. It sloped down to a ditch of stagnant water below.

"They can't run us off the public highway," said Ma. "Highway belongs to everybody, I reckon."

"No grass for the hosses," said Big Joe.

"Stake 'em up yonder," said Pa. "Looks a mite better there. Little Jeff, you and me's goin' over to that thicket and hunt us up some wood."

"*Po*-lice can't run us off if we're sleepin', can they, Ma?" asked Trixie.

"I'd like to see 'em try it," said Ma.

Soon a campfire was burning, throwing sparks up in the

night sky. Ma put a skillet on the fire, mixed some dough and threw in some grease. In a few minutes large round cakes of dough were sizzling. Pa and Big Joe ate first. Then they left to walk down to the gas station at the next corner. "I'll ask about cotton to pick," said Pa.

Trixie and Little Jeff crouched down by the fire. The light shone on their faces and threw big shadows across the road. Granny on her box began to sing her made-up tune:

"Sleepin' in the churchyard,
Underneath the trees,
I'll listen to the birdies sing
And feel the gentle breeze . . ."

Suddenly Trixie screamed: "PO-LICE!" Her scream faded away, and her mouth remained open, as she pointed.

"Who is it?" asked Ma, turning quickly. "Mr. Bryce again?"

Trixie ran to her mother. "It's that boy, George, and Jim, the storekeeper," she said.

Ma stepped forward boldly. "*Now* what? We gotta move on again?"

"How you folks doin'?" asked Jim Harter. "All right?"

Ma Medley gulped. The man's voice was friendly. "Sure," she said.

"I brought you some stuff," said Jim. He leaned over to put down some cans of beans and milk and three loaves of bread.

"We've got rations," said Ma stiffly. "We brung stuff from home."

43

"I know," said Jim Harter, "but I thought . . ."

"We got money, we'll pay you . . ."

"Better keep it till . . ."

"But why should *you* . . ." began Ma.

Ma and Jim were groping toward an understanding.

"They was so afraid you'd mess up their purty church-house," said Jim Harter.

"But that's no reason . . . why you should give us . . ." said Ma. "It's the purtiest church-house ever I did see. I don't blame 'em for not wantin' it messed up. I took one look in at the door . . ." then hastily, "but I didn't touch nary a thing."

Granny's head was nodding. Her chin sank down on her breast, as she fell asleep.

The boy George walked up to Ma Medley. "I thought you was dirty people," he said.

"It's hard to keep clean without plenty of water," said Ma.

"I told 'em you-all was goin' to visit your kinfolk," said Jim Harter, "but they wouldn't listen."

A scuffle broke out. Ma turned to see Trixie and Little Jeff fighting. "What you doin'?" she called out. "Stop it!"

"This-here George called us gypsies and thieves!" shouted Trixie.

"We're a-beatin' him up," shouted Little Jeff.

It was a fierce fight while it lasted. Jim Harter tore the children apart.

"I'll learn him to call us names," said Little Jeff.

George wiped a bloody nose. Whimpering, he ran behind the storekeeper for protection.

"Can I do anything for you-all?" Jim Harter asked.

"Jest tell us where we can git water," said Ma. "We don't like to bother the folks in this town. Some folks won't even give you water. We always stop at the poorest houses. Poor people are bigger-hearted."

"There's a pump right by my store," said Jim. "I'll send George back with a bucketful." The two disappeared in the darkness. A little later, George brought the water, set it down, and left without a word.

When Pa and Big Joe returned from the gas station, Pa said, "No use. We gotta go farther south tomorrow. Man said they got too many pickers here, with all them Mexicans. No grass neither."

"Let's go to bed then," said Ma, "so we can git up early and leave at sunrise."

Pa and Big Joe spread the mattresses under the wagons. They all stretched out and pulled up their quilts. Cars passed and people stared. Curious people walked by on the highway, but did not speak. They all slept but Ma. She watched the stars for a long time. Then, worn out with weariness, she too dropped off to sleep.

The next morning when George and the school children passed on their way to school, the camping place was empty. A blackened spot showed where the campfire had been. Bent weeds showed where the horses had been tethered. That was all. No tin cans or torn paper littered the roadside. There was nothing to tell that a lonely family had slept there on cornshuck mattresses, with two wagon-beds over them for shelter.

It was a week later when the Medleys came back, driving northward. When the little caravan passed the schoolyard, all the children lined up, staring.

"There's them gypsies!" cried George. "They're mean fighters. That boy gave me a bloody nose."

But the people on the wagons did not look or hear. Big Joe slapped the lines on the gray horse's back and Pa Medley called *giddap* to the team. Old Granny hummed her hymn-tunes contentedly. Little Jeff pulled gently on the rope to keep the pony moving.

"There's that purty church-house," said Ma. "*Promised Land,* they call it."

"We don't want to stop here," said Pa.

" 'Promised Land?' Be this the place they call 'Promised Land?' " asked Granny. "The land of milk and honey?"

"It would be nice to see inside that church-house again," said Ma, "but I wouldn't go near it now. Not even if they asked me to. Let's keep goin' . . ."

But they had to stop, for there was Jim Harter running out of his store and hailing them.

"You folks all right?" he asked.

"Sure," said Ma. It was good to see his friendly face.

"We didn't find no steady cotton-pickin'," said Pa. "Most of 'em said they had plenty pickers and didn't need us."

"Did you want to pick cotton?" asked Jim Harter in astonishment.

"We sure did," said Ma. "We heard over the radio back home, that they needed hundreds of cotton pickers in this county in Arkansas. So we thought we'd come down from the hills and pick a while. We aimed to camp out if we couldn't git us a house — the nights is so warm."

"One man give us a job and told us to sleep in his storm-cellar," said Pa. "But we ruther sleep up top o' the ground."

"There was snakes in that-'ere cellar," piped up Trixie. "I was a-scared."

"That man, he hired everybody that come along," said Ma. "He hired so many pickers, they got his cotton picked in one day. So our job was soon over." It was good to talk over troubles with a friend.

"I picked twenty pounds," announced Trixie.

"I done picked eleven," said Little Jeff.

"If I'd a known you wanted to pick cotton," Jim Harter said, "I coulda got you a job right here. My brother-in-law was lookin' for cotton-pickers. I didn't like to ask you what you was after. I figgered it wasn't none o' my business."

"They wouldn't a hired us after . . . what happened in the churchyard," said Pa. "They thought we was bums . . . bad people . . . but the Lord knows . . ."

"If I'd a known, I coulda spoke to . . ." began Jim again. He turned to Ma. "You folks needin' anything? Bread or milk or any other stuff?"

Ma smiled. "Thank you," she said. "We got enough to git us back home. We'll go back to the hills and stay there."

Jim Harter stood by awkwardly, then he looked down at Trixie. "Come over to the store a minute," he said. She put her hand in his and walked with him.

When Trixie came back, she was sucking hard on a stick of candy. She took another stick out of a paper sack and handed it to Little Jeff. They climbed up on the wagon with Ma. Big

Joe and Pa slapped the lines on the horses' backs. Little Jeff pulled gently on the pony's rope. They all waved good-by to Jim Harter.

The little caravan passed the country church, but no one looked at it. It went slowly up the road and disappeared in the distance.

Mary Silver

Elizabeth Coatsworth

It was late afternoon of an August day in 1725 and the Indian village of Saint Francis was filled with the stir of many returns: men returning from hunting and women from their work in the cornfields at the edge of the forest; even the children came running singly and in groups up from the Chaudière River where they had been swimming and fishing or helping with the drying of the many eels that lay on the clean pebbles and the racks. The kettles in the long bark houses were boiling and sinewy hands stretched toward the wooden bowls to fill them with succotash and venison.

Kanaskwa, the slave, was braiding her hair with an eelskin dyed scarlet. Except for its red and the bright blue of her eyes, she seemed in the dusky firelight of the long house like a girl made of doeskin: brown hair, brown face, and brown fringed dress and leggings were all much of one color. She was nearly fifteen, tall and wellmade, but not pretty. It was for her voice that she was known in the village and valued by her master, Sawatis — that voice which sounded like a brook when she spoke and like a bird when she sang.

She was singing now to herself, a ritual song:

Deep the dew-water falls,
No one comes close to me!
Where are you, whippoorwill?
Why am I waiting now,
Calling you, calling you?

"Come, the kettle is hot," said her mistress.

Kanaskwa swung her newly plaited braids in place with a quick movement of her head and turned toward the fire where Sawatis and his family were already seated on their blankets at one end of the room which had three doors, and sheltered three families. But before the girl could move forward a child darted in at another entrance.

"Kanaskwa," he said urgently, but in a low voice. "Quick! The soldiers are coming for you again!"

Even as he spoke the girl turned and ran toward the nearest door, but as she pushed aside the deerskin over the entrance a tall young man in an English uniform entered, almost colliding with her, and before she could twist past him, caught her firmly by the wrist.

"Aha, my little fox!" he exclaimed in the Indian tongue. "Now we have you, I think."

Blue eyes looked into gray for an instant, then the girl tore her wrist free by a sudden fierce motion and whirled, only to be caught at the shoulder by a hand swift as her own and pulled back.

The Indians had not stirred from the blankets where they sat. They were eating as though nothing had happened.

Abruptly Kanaskwa gave up the struggle and stood quietly with expressionless face.

"That is better, wild cat," said the young man. "As far as I am concerned you could stay with the Indians forever, but the gentlemen in Boston have different ideas." He turned to her master. "I am sent by the commission again, Sawatis, and have brought the customary redemption money with me," he said, "though really you don't deserve it for the number of times you have hidden this girl even though you knew the French governor himself had ordered her return to her family."

Sawatis looked at him quietly. "How are we to know of the affairs of Quebec? I go on hunting trips now and then in the forest and the slave goes with me. But she is worth more than you have given: she is good with the corn and dresses a doeskin well. Besides that she sings. Kanaskwa, sing that we may hear you."

"I will not sing for these white thieves," answered the girl.

"You will do as I command," said her master.

Kanaskwa shrugged her shoulders wearily, and staring at the fire began to sing, making no effort to sing well, but her voice was beautiful in spite of her, and the house was filled with the low haunting music, so that the Indians at their fires stopped what they were doing to listen to her, and the soldiers in the doors forgot their grinning, and a softness came over the gray eyes of Colonel Caleb Greene.

Catching the darkness up,
I hear the Eagle-bird
Pulling the blanket back
From the east, sleeping still.

51

> *How swift he flies, bearing the sun*
>   *to the morning!*

When she was silent, Colonel Caleb cleared his throat. He was a very young officer, just past his twentieth birthday.

"You are right, Sawatis," he said. "Here's another pound out of my own pocket. But not another penny," he added, as the Indian opened his mouth to protest. "Don't forget I have the governor's warrant for fetching home Mary Silver, called Kanaskwa, the slave, and soldiers to carry it out. There's a new peace between France and England."

The Indian grinned and struck hands on the bargain.

"She's a good girl, but needs the stick," he remarked philosophically.

"Come along, Mary Silver," said Colonel Caleb. "If you have anything to bring with you, hurry and get it ready."

"I have nothing" she answered.

Her mistress came to her side with a blanket of wolfskins.

"Take this with you my daughter," she said with tears in her eyes. "Long shall I miss you in the field and in the lodge and in all the tasks of the day."

"Oh, do not let them take me, my mother," cried the girl suddenly with a sob.

"We can do nothing, my child," said the woman. "May thy road be straight. Farewell."

"Farewell," said Kanaskwa, holding up her head. "I shall never forget you. Some day I shall come back."

She looked about once at the Indians who looked at her, a long look from many pairs of black eyes that seemed to be saying:

"We shall be waiting. Come back to the corn and the forests. Come back, Kanaskwa."

Colonel Caleb made a gesture and the girl walked to the door, and out into the dusk of the village, while a soldier stepped to each side of her and laid a hand on her arm. The village was almost deserted, but from within the houses she heard the voices that she knew so well, and from beyond the willows sounded the great waterfall that had sung day and night in her ears.

Canoes with paddlers waited for them at the landing beach. Not until they were well out in the river did the hands leave her arms. The men talked together in French which she could not understand, as they paddled from the Chaudière into the wide current of the Saint Lawrence, and slowly the sunset light faded out of the sky, and the evening star shone in the west and then one by one the great constellations appeared. No one paid any attention to her, sitting in the center of the canoe, a prisoner among strangers, until at last Colonel Caleb turned about and spoke cheerfully. As she did not answer, he looked closely into her face in the starlight.

"Why, my child, you're shivering," he said in the Indian. "You would think we were enemies! It is to your own mother I am taking you, Mary Silver."

In the dim light she looked back at him, fearful and hostile. Did she not know what awaited her, never again to be allowed to step foot outdoors, to be tied into clothes that were a torture, and beaten because she did not know how to bake bread and pray as the Boston people prayed? Had not the Indians often told her?

If she was to be illtreated, Colonel Caleb was slow to begin, waiting, she felt sure, until he had her away from Quebec and entirely at his mercy. Here there was still a chance that someone might rescue her and send her back to the Indians, but in the French town no one paid any attention to a blue-eyed girl in Indian clothes, for Indian prisoners were no rarity. Colonel Caleb took her to an inn where the innkeeper's wife bathed her and dressed her in European clothes and did up her hair under a French cap.

Then she took her down to Colonel Caleb in the inn parlor.

"Now, sir, where is your Indian girl?" she asked.

"Bless us," said the colonel, "I would never have known you, Mary Silver. Will you dine with me this evening?"

There was a twinkle in his eye as he looked at her. He was making fun of her, playing with her because she was in his power.

She met his look with her blazing blue eyes.

"A squaw does not eat with braves," she said.

"We are not squaws and braves, Mary Silver," he answered, his eyes twinkling more than ever.

Surely his apparent good nature was only to put her off her guard. She looked at him, defiant and forlorn.

"Kanaskwa!" he said sharply. "I am your master now. Sit down as I have bidden you." And the girl sat down. "Eat!" he said, and she ate, watching him carefully to see how he used his knife and fork and spoon and then making no mistakes.

He tried to talk, but she would not respond.

"I am to get your brother Nathaniel tomorrow," he said at last.

She could not keep the look of interest out of her eyes. Did she really have a brother, she wondered, or was he lying to her for some reason she did not understand.

"He has been as hard to get as you," Colonel Caleb went on. "This is the third time I have been here to Quebec after you two. Sawatis always got wind of my arrival and took to the woods; and the Tardieus, the French people who bought Nathaniel from the Indians soon after he was captured, claimed that the boy was dead. They had him hidden in Montreal, but I heard of it. And tomorrow the governor has commanded that he be brought here."

Dinner was finished and he folded his arms and sat looking into the fire. Kanaskwa watched him. He was one of the Boston men whom the Indians said were liars and thieves, all treacherous and cruel. He did not look to be these things, but young, courageous, and kind. Even so, she was prepared to believe the worst of him. For Indian stories told of being deceived by fine words and appearances, following some magician met in the forest and being lost forever. Perhaps the Boston men were like that.

She had almost forgotten that she, herself, was of their race.

The next morning she woke early in her high room, and glanced about, astonished to be alone, for she was accustomed to the Indian encampments where everyone — men, women, and children — slept crowded close together. She ran to the door, but it was, as she knew, locked on the outside. She ran to the little window, but she could only see a handful of sky and a bit of cobbled street below and the crowded houses opposite. The smells and the sounds were different. She was sick with homesickness for the things she knew and the ways to which she was accustomed. Here not a bird sang, not a breeze stirred in the trees; she was trapped, betrayed, and miserable.

She walked lightly about the room, testing the door to see if she might open it, examining the narrow window and the roof to see if there were a possible means of escape. In the darkness of the night before, when the landlady had brought her back to her room, she had taken off the French clothes and dressed herself again in her doeskin trimmed with beads and dyed porcupine quills. She had slept on the floor on the wolfskin blanket, disdaining the softness of the bed. How alone she felt, uprooted from the forest and river!

For several hours she stood by the little window looking out and watching, concentrating all her restlessness on the perceptions of her senses. In the middle of the morning, she saw approaching a boy about two years younger than herself, accompanied by soldiers. Her heart gave a great leap. She had seen her own reflection often enough in pools and kettles of water and was sure that this boy looked like her, but younger and less reserved. Surely this was Nathaniel, her brother, and at last she had someone who belonged to her.

In a short time Colonel Caleb sent the landlady to fetch Kanaskwa down. She exclaimed upon seeing the girl again in her Indian clothes. The colonel also gave a laugh at seeing her.

"Good morning, Kanaskwa," he exclaimed. "Here is your brother Nathaniel," and then speaking in French said to the boy, "and this is your sister Mary who has lived with the Indians."

The two looked at one another eagerly but there was an awkwardness between them, a brother and sister who could speak no word of each other's language.

"But soon," the boy said, smiling eagerly, "we shall be embracing our own mother, and already I have a dear sister!"

As he spoke, he moved his hands rapidly like a Frenchman, trying to express his meaning, which Colonel Caleb was forced to translate. Kanaskwa smiled at him sadly.

"I shall go back!" she murmured.

"Eat your breakfast, children," the colonel said in two languages. "Now that you are both here, the sooner we get over the formalities and sail, the better."

From the deck of the sloop, *Perseverance*, Mary Silver, still in her Indian clothes, disconsolately watched Quebec fade from sight and the distant shores of the river slip by as they sailed down with the tide. It seemed as though she had always known those mountains and that great river and the dark forests along its banks. She thought of jumping overboard and trying to swim to shore, but Colonel Caleb's eyes were on her, and besides, she knew that she would never reach the bank. Nathaniel was soon helping the sailors, running errands, hauling rope, taking his turn at the tiller, but Mary Silver stood looking at no one, watching always the land they were leaving. She started and winced at a touch on her shoulder.

It was Colonel Caleb again, who sat down on the rail near her, one boot swinging.

"Tell me," he said, "why do you love the Indians? I have spent several years at the trading posts, and have acted often as interpreter among them. I understand their customs. Now, it is usual when taking prisoners, especially children, to adopt them into the tribe. Why were you not adopted? Why do they still call you Kanaskwa, the slave, after ten years?"

The girl hid her face.

"Answer, Kanaskwa!" he said with authority.

"I would not!" she exclaimed. "They had killed my father.

57

I can remember him lying on the ground, stripped and bleeding. I would not be adopted!"

"And yet," he exclaimed, "you fought like a wild cat to stay with them!"

"That is different," she flashed back. "I am afraid to go to the white people. My heart is sick for the things I know — "

She stopped, looking at him desperately.

"You are a fool, Mary Silver!" he said. "All your life with the Indians you have been beaten and made to do the heaviest work because you could not forget a dead father, and now when the chance comes to go back to your mother and your own kin, you sicken and grieve for these same men who killed him! You are too loyal, or not loyal enough! You walk with your eyes on the trail behind you! Look forward, Mary Silver, and take hope!"

"It is not in my head," she whispered, "it is in my heart where words cannot reach."

Every day Colonel Caleb talked to her of New England, trying to interest her and make her forget Saint Francis.

"You will like milking the cows," he said.

"Do they live in the house?" she asked.

"No," he answered, smiling, "they have their byres in the winter and in the summer they stay in the fields."

"But I shall not be allowed to go to the fields."

"What foolish talk is this?" he exclaimed. "When your work is done you may go abroad as much as you like, I warrant."

She shook her head, her face turned toward the northwest whence she had come.

It was a fine bright day when they sailed into the quiet water of Pemaquid Harbor. The gulls were making a great commotion with the outgoing tide and a kingfisher scolded at them from a dead oak tree. Nathaniel exclaimed with delight over everything, bidding a warm but hasty good-bye to the crew.

They spent the night at the tavern near the fort and in the morning hired three horses.

The farm where Mrs. Silver lived with Jacob Rising, her brother, was twenty miles away. Colonel Caleb would not be back at Pemaquid until the next night, but the *Perseverance* was to wait for him.

As far as she could remember, Mary Silver had never ridden a horse, but she was strong and supple and learned as soon as her brother the management of her mount.

With the motion of that strong body under her, and the joy of solid land beneath them and forest about them, an unthinking wildness seized the girl, and half in an access of gayety and half in earnest, she urged her horse to a canter. If she could only outrun the others and follow the hunting trails north and north until she got back to the Indian village.

But Colonel Caleb's horse overtook hers. His hand was on the bridle.

"You will tire your poor beast," he said with a grim smile. "I gave you the old horse, Kanaskwa."

But even if she could not escape, she could be happy for a little while, and she rode singing the Indian songs that she knew, while the other two listened amazed as always by the beauty of her voice.

By evening, when they came to the clearings of the Sheepscot, she was tired. Colonel Caleb inquired the way, and faces peered up at them as they sat in their saddles.

"Aye, they favor the Rising side of the family," said the woman of the house where they had inquired. "This will be a happy day for Alice Silver when her children come home."

"Aye, a happy day," said Colonel Caleb.

Now they had come to a farm running down to the river, and a man unfastened his oxen from a cart, waved to them, and hurried toward the house, leaving the patient animals standing where they were. The door of the farmhouse opened and a woman ran out at the sound of the hoofs.

"Oh, my children! My children! Thank God you are come home!" she cried. "Mary! Nathaniel!" — she began weeping and laughing, holding up her arms in the dusk as they slipped from their saddles to kiss her.

"Mother!" said Nathaniel — and the girl murmured something in Indian.

By this time their uncle had run up.

"A fine-looking pair of colts," he said to Colonel Caleb. "Now there'll be youth in the house, and my sister will have her own again!"

For a little while the bustle covered the awkwardness, but when they all sat down at the trestle table, it seemed strange that there were mother, daughter, and son, no one of whom could talk to any of the others. Colonel Caleb, who seemed preoccupied, acted as interpreter, but after a while conversation lagged. Everything — the blessing at the table, the food, the clothes, the furniture, the very feel of the air — was unknown to Mary Silver. She felt her heart sinking and sinking. At dawn Colonel Caleb would go. Then she would be like a deaf and dumb person until she had learned this rumbling speech.

Something moved its sinuous length along the hearth and

Mary caught up the poker, but her uncle seized her arm, while everyone laughed.

"It is only an animal like a dog," explained the colonel. "It is called a cat and feeds on milk."

She dropped the poker, crimsoning with shame at having made herself ridiculous.

"They are very like the wild cats in the woods," added the colonel quickly, "and everyone knows, my sister, that *they* are dangerous."

Mary Silver shot him a grateful look from her blue eyes. Bedtime came early, for though the mother would gladly have looked at her redeemed children for hours, even she could see that they were almost exhausted.

When the girl said good night to Colonel Caleb, she added in a low voice: "My older brother, before we part, forgive me for all the trouble I have caused you."

"You have more than made up for any trouble, child," he exclaimed warmly. "But I shall see you before I go in the morning? And I'll visit you often — now that we are friends."

"You are good," she said very low and before he could speak again, she had slipped silently out behind her mother who led the way with a lighted candle.

But Mary Silver was determined that by morning she would be far from that place on her way to freedom. This gentle, kind-faced woman was her mother, yet she could remember nothing of her: she was no more than a stranger. Mary had been stolen when she was six years old. Her mother had chanced to be at a neighbor's on an errand. Mary could remember seeing the sheep huddle together in a corner of the field and hearing her father say, "What ails the beasts, I

61

wonder?" She remembered his dead body. That was all of her old life: there remained no memory of house and hearth, of spinning wheel and stable to make her return easier for her and to deaden her longing for the hard, casual, dangerous life she knew so well.

She could hear voices below as she knelt by the window in the room they had given her. When all were asleep she would steal out of the house and follow the north star toward the Penobscot. She would take food and in three or four days she would come on Indian villages where she could make herself known. She would go with the next party up the river toward the Saint Lawrence and perhaps in a few weeks, at any rate by spring, she would be back at Saint Francis.

Outside the summer night was full of the sound of crickets. The stars wheeled slowly westward and a loon gave its melancholy cry from the river. She could hear the cattle moving a little in their stalls in the barn beyond the ell and the stamping of a horse.

A woman's voice was singing, softly and happily, a foolish old song:

> *"Alas! my love, you do me wrong*
> *To cast me off discourteously,*
> *And I have loved you so long,*
> *Delighting in your company.*
> *Green-sleeves was all my joy,*
> *Green-sleeves was my delight. . . . "*

Mary Silver did not understand the words, but the tune she understood. It brought back all the past. Suddenly she remembered a world of things, of lying in her mother's arms while her mother sang, of her doll Betsy who had fallen down the well, of Spot, the old hound, and yellow Grizel the cow, all these came back, the singing, the spinning wheel, safety and love. Now everything that had happened since seemed like a dream and lost its importance. The tears choked her — all her stoicism melted in a tender sorrow to the sound of her mother's singing; the last fear and distrust, the last memory of the lies that the Indians had told her flowed away with her tears.

There was much that her mind did not understand, but suddenly, unexpectedly, her heart was at home.

Once in the Year

Elizabeth Yates

When supper was over, Martha and Andrew put on their warm coats. Andrew pulled his cap down over his ears and Martha threw a woolen shawl over her head and tied it under her chin. Laughter was in their voices and lightness in their movements, for this was one time when care could be set aside. The animals had been fed early and bedded down for the night so that Andrew had no worries for them; and Martha had spent the whole week cooking and cleaning so her mind was free from household chores. Her husband and her son, and Benj who had been part of the farm for so many years, would not want for anything that was hers to give them for days to come.

"You'll be asleep when we get back," Andrew said, just as they were going out the door, "so the next greeting we'll be giving you will be Merry Christmas."

Martha's eyes twinkled. Even the plain words said every night of the year, "Good-night, Peter," seemed so much more meaningful when the next ones would be "Merry Christmas!"

Then they called good-by and stepped out into the frosty night.

Peter ran to the window and pushed the curtain aside to watch them. Arm in arm they went over the path, two black figures on the white field of snow, with stars looking down on them and the dark lines of the hills rimming them in a known world. Now they were running a little, then they stopped as if to catch their breath and Peter saw his mother toss her head quickly, then his father threw back his head and laughed.

What a wonderful time Christmas Eve was, Peter thought, the world so still and everyone in it so happy. For so many days of the year his father was serious and full of care and his mother's thoughts seemed far ahead of her as if she were thinking of all the things she had to do; but tonight they were gay and lighthearted.

When Peter could see them no longer, he returned to the circle of warmth by the stove. Benj was sitting there, gazing dreamily into the coals. Peter brought up a stool and sat beside him. It might be beautiful outside and great things might be going on in the village, but here it was warm and the deep wonder of the night was as much within the familiar kitchen as it was outdoors in the starlit quiet.

"Tell me a story, Benj. Tell me about Christmas, how it all happened," Peter said.

Peter knew it well but he wanted to hear it again, and though the story itself did not change, Benj never failed to add something new at the end.

Benj nodded slowly and began to tell Peter the old story of the stable at Bethlehem, of the man and woman who had found shelter there because there was no room at the inn, and of the ox and the ass who had moved aside a little to share their place with the travelers.

"And out on the hillside there were shepherds with their sheep," Benj went on, "some of them talking around a bit of a fire they had made, holding out their hands to warm them for there was a chill on the air that night; and some of them had gone to sleep. But, of a sudden, the night about them became white with light. They looked up to see where the light came from and it was as if the very doors of heaven had opened to them. Then they heard an angel telling them what had happened."

"What had happened, Benj? What made the night turn to light?"

"In that stable yonder in Bethlehem a child had been born to the woman. He it was that the ages had been waiting for. He it was who would bring true light to the world, and though he would not do it as a child, nor yet as a young man, and though the world would stumble on in its darkness for many years until he came to the fullness of his manhood, there was light that night of his birth. A kind of sign it was of what his coming into the world meant, and the darkness would never be so dark again."

Benj was seeing it all, as clearly as had the shepherds on that far away hillside, and his eyes were shining.

"The shepherds left their flocks in charge of their dogs and went to the stable to see the child. A fine strong boy he was. They brought food in their pouches to share with the man and the woman, and when they returned to the hillside they were not hungry, for the joy they bore with them fed them as heartily as the bread and the cheese they had left behind. After a while the night grew quiet again. Midnight came. The family were alone in the stable. And then — , " Benj breathed deeply, as if recalling something so marvelous that there might not be words to tell of it, "a wonderful thing happened."

"What was it, Benj?" Peter asked. The story had been familiar to him up to this point but now it was new.

"In that dark stillness, unbroken by even a baby's crying, the creatures in the stable began to talk among themselves — the great slow-moving ox, and the tired little ass, a half-grown sheep that had followed the shepherds to Bethlehem, and a brown hen who had roosted in the rafters at sundown. They talked together and to the child."

"Didn't they talk to the others — the man and the woman?"

Benj shook his head. "Those two had gone to sleep." He looked at Peter and spoke slowly. "It's said that on every Christmas Eve, near midnight and for a while after, the creatures talk among themselves. It is the only time they do so, the only time of the year."

"Can anyone hear them, Benj?"

The old man shook his head again. "Only the still of heart, for only they will listen long enough to catch the meaning of so strange a sound."

"Have you heard them, Benj?"

"I have, Peter, times without number, and they always say the same thing."

"What do they say?"

"I cannot tell you now. What they say to me might be very different from what they would say to anyone else."

Peter looked at the clock. The hands were at nine. Such a long way it was to midnight, yet he knew that somehow he must stay awake to hear the creatures talk together.

A while later Benj banked the stove, lowered the lamp and said good-night to Peter. Peter went upstairs to bed and Benj went out to the barn to make his nightly rounds. The animals were safe and contented, he knew, but this was one night when he must be doubly sure, tired though his limbs might be from the work of the day.

The quietness of night enveloped the farmhouse, enveloped the world; but the night was unlike any other, for wonder was abroad and there was an air of expectancy that beggared sleep.

Up in his room, Peter heard the clock strike eleven, then he heard the laughter of his mother and the well-known tones of his father's voice as they came up the path from the village. Their voices lowered as they entered the house and talked together in the kitchen, warming their hands by the stove. Quietly they came up the stairs and stood outside Peter's door, then the door was pushed open a crack.

"He's asleep," Andrew said.

"Good, then we haven't wakened him," Martha added. She would have liked to cross the room and tuck his covers in, but she would not risk waking him at such an hour and the next day Christmas.

Peter lay very still, his eyelids trembling as he kept them closed over his eyes. What would his mother say if she came over to the bed and saw that he had not undressed — that he had put a stone under his pillow so discomfort would keep him awake? The door closed and his parents tiptoed into their own room. There were small sounds and whispers, a bit of soft laughter, then stillness and the ticking of the kitchen clock telling Peter that its hands were drawing near midnight.

Slowly, one foot then another, he got out of bed and put on

his coat that had been made from the wool of Biddy's last shearing. He took his shoes in his hands and crept down the stairs to the kitchen. Peering up into the face of the clock he saw the hands at a quarter to twelve. He sat down on the floor to put on his shoes. Going to the door he opened it noiselessly and closed it behind him, then ran lightly to the barn.

It was very still in the barn and very dark, but as his eyes became used to the darkness he could discern dimly the familiar shapes of the farm animals in their chosen positions of sleep. The barn seemed strange so near the mid hour of night and Peter, to assure himself, went to each animal in turn, to caress them and feel the comfort of their knowing presences.

First, there was the black yearling, Biddy's last lamb, who was growing to be the flock's leader. Peter slipped into the pen where the sheep were folded and whistled softly. The yearling shook itself out of sleep and came over to the boy, rubbing against him and eating the raw potato Peter had brought in his pocket.

Then Peter went to the stall where his father's work horse stood. The horse whinnied and reached for the lump of sugar Peter offered.

Then he went to the stanchions where the cows were, all three of them lying with their legs tucked under them and chewing their cuds peacefully. Peter stroked each gentle head and took the rhythmic sound of chewing as their sufficient greeting.

Going over to the corner where the hens roosted for the night, he looked up at them.

"Hello," he said. "It's just Peter. Don't be alarmed."

They moved on their perch ever so lightly and started talking among themselves, soft sounds as if they were so far asleep they could bear to be wakened but still must let Peter know that they were aware of his presence and were glad for it.

Peter found a pile of hay near the horse's stall and curled up in it to listen to the creatures when midnight came. He was hardly settled when from far down in the valley the village clock could be heard. Peter held his breath as twelve strokes resounded on the night with slow and measured import. While their echo faded, the same stillness filled the barn that had been there when Peter first entered; but it was only for a moment. Soon it was broken by a rustle of straw here, and a stamp of a hoof there, a single deep-toned baa-aa, a short neigh, and chickens cooing in their sleep.

Almost before Peter realized what had happened, he was caught up in a conversation the creatures were having. It was an old story they were telling, as far as he could make out, one the horse had heard as a colt from his dam, and long before that it had first been told by a small weary ass. It was a story the cow had heard as a calf and which had been first told by an ox in a stable in Judea. It was a story that the sheep knew because all sheep heard it from their ewes when they were lambs. It was a story that a single brown hen had left as a heritage for all hens. And they told it again, each in a way peculiar to cow, horse, sheep, hen, as if to remind themselves of why this night was hallowed.

"I had worked all day," the cow said, thinking for that moment that she was the ox and might speak as such. "I had drawn heavy loads and knocked my feet against the rough stones in the fields, but when the child was born and all that light shone in my stable the work I had done seemed a beautiful thing and the thought of it no longer tired me. It was the light that made me see we were born to serve so One on high might rule."

"Oh, I was weary, too," the horse said, and his voice became small and plaintive as he fancied himself the ass. "We had journeyed so far that day, so very far, and mind you, as it turned out, it was two I had been carrying, not just one. My head drooped so low that I thought I could never lift it again and even the hay in the manger did not interest me. Then came that light and everything was different. I felt so humble in its glow that I did not care if I never raised my head again. And I was glad my back was strong to bear burdens and that my feet could be sure, no matter how rough the way. I was glad, too, that man had use for me, for serving him brought me closer to the God he serves."

"I was not weary or burdened," the black yearling spoke up, thinking he was the half-grown lamb that had followed in the wake of the shepherds. "I had been grazing all day and when darkness came and the flock had been folded I had tucked my legs under me to sleep. Then the light appeared. It was such a dazzling thing it took away from me all thinking. There were no thoughts in my head, such as 'Shall I stay? Shall I go?' There was only one compelling desire and it drew me to the stable where I stayed. I saw my shepherd giving his pouch of food to the mother and I thought then, 'Take what I have and use it, it is all for glory.' "

One of the hens shook her feathers and came down from the roost. The sound of her voice was sweetly melodious, as if the feathered creatures of the world in making her their spokesman had loaned her the gift of song.

"I said to myself, 'This is a very great moment. How shall I praise God for letting me be here?' There was only one thing

71

to do. I nestled down in the straw and laid an egg so when it came time for the night's fast to be broken there would be something for hungry folk to eat. And so, ever since that time long ago, an egg has been our way of praise. It is our highest gift."

The rustling in the straw ceased. The hen's slow sleepy movements on the roost were over. Not so much as the stamp of a hoof or the muffled baa-ing of a sheep broke the stillness in the barn. Peter rubbed his eyes in astonishment. He had heard the creatures talking on Christmas Eve, talking of what had taken place on the first Christmas Eve.

He knew something now of what dwelt behind the quietness in the soft eyes of horse and cow, the gentle gaze of the sheep, and the cool glance of the hen. They had never forgotten the time when they had been of use, and remembering it had marked their lives with blessing. Like a shining thread running down the ages, it gave meaning and dignity to the work each one did. Love had made them wise that night, lightening every labor they might do thereafter.

There was a stir among the dark shadows of the barn and Peter saw old Benj coming to stand beside him. It was too dark to see his face, but his form and his footsteps were unmistakable. Peter had thought he was alone in the barn, but it did not surprise him to know that Benj had been there, too.

"I heard them talking together," Peter whispered excitedly. "Did you hear them, Benj — ,"

"Aye, I heard them," the old man nodded.

"It was wonderful what they said, wasn't it, Benj?"

"Wonderful, indeed."

Peter took Benj's hand and the two started back to the house across the white barnyard under the star-decked sky.

"It's the same for us as it is for them, isn't it, Benj?"

"Aye, it's the same for us as we all serve the one Father, but only the still of heart can catch that message and link it to their lives."

A few minutes later Peter was ready to close his eyes in sleep, when he smiled to himself in the darkness of his room. Christmas seemed a more beautiful time than it had ever seemed before — a time when one gave of one's best and rejoiced in the giving because it was one's all.

And then, it was almost as if his mother were standing beside his bed for he could hear her talking to him; but it was not her words, it was the words her mother had used when Martha was a little girl.

"When something wonderful happens to people on Christmas Eve, it is to be cherished in the heart and in the mind. We must not be afraid of the wonderful things, nor must we let others laugh them away from us. Only thus do we learn to hold our dreams — "

Peter smiled to himself again, then he turned his head on his pillow and went to sleep.

A Tale of the Poplar

Charles Boardman Hawes

McMaster wanted poplar, and McLaren cut it. It came down to the dam, and lay so thick in the dead water, where the river spreads to half a mile in breadth, that neither canoe nor *bateau* could pass. So men carried their canoes round the blockade and beached their *bateaux* above; and McLaren stormed because his crews were idle at Number 12. But McMaster was intent on three big lumber deals, and by his orders the "popple" was held indefinitely. It floated on the river day after day until frosts came and puddles froze, and the mud along the edge of the river was crusted on top by the cold. At last McLaren put his crews to work trying to finish a new camp before the first snow.

François Latteau was an artist with the birch-bark horn. For seven years he had worked for McLaren, and each year the same thing had happened. On an October afternoon François would sit down at the summit of the ridge with a great sheet of white bark; he would trim the bark with his keen knife, shape it and bend it, and make it tight with pitch, until he had a long, tapering instrument shaped like a megaphone, with a narrow mouth.

Toward dusk he would go down to the little lake four miles away, where deep woods enclosed the sandy beach and shoals of lily pads; there he would put the bark horn to his lips and utter a long, wailing cry, which began very low, and rose and fell and rose again, until it died away and left all the lake ringing with the echo. As he gave the call, François would wave the end of the horn back and forth and in circles, at first close to the ground, then high in the air, then near the ground again. When he waved the horn an odd quaver came into the call; when the mouth of the horn was near the ground the call was low and muffled; but when the horn was up and pointed into the air it became a full-throated cry that blared into the solitude and silence.

The men said that François Latteau could call a moose from Mount Katahdin to Suncook Lake by the magic of his voice, and that he inherited the trick from his grandfather, a Penobscot chief.

Very often, as François squatted by the shore of the lake, an answering call would come from valley or ridge or swamp far off among the hills. Then François Latteau would be cautious; hiding under the overhanging brush, he would call, and call again. As the answer came nearer and nearer, now clear as a bugle note, now muffled by intervening ridges, he would change the tone, and occasionally give little grunts and whining sounds that were not unlike the whimper of a hungry dog. At the same time he would stir the water with a stick, and make a noise that was like the splash of a cow feeding in the lily pads. François Latteau was exceptionally clever at this art; he had in his time killed a great many moose.

As the men sat round the camp in the evenings they used to

75

imitate his moose call. François would smile scornfully at their efforts; and afterward, when the men went out to the pond and tried to call moose in earnest, they had no luck.

Barney Osborne seldom tried the moose call; he always sat in silence, listening to the others. Sometimes, however, when the men were telling stories in the evening, he would furtively clasp his hands and hoot so much like an owl that even François Latteau would start in surprise. Barney was a good mimic, and more than once, when François gave the moose call, he had watched every move of the Frenchman, and marked every cadence of the eerie call.

When, with the passing of October, the season for moose came in, François Latteau made a new horn, and the men looked forward to a banquet of moose meat.

The new camp on which they were working was five miles beyond the river, and every day, as they went back and forth to their work by way of the dam, they saw the poplar lying in the dead water.

Early on a Saturday afternoon they started back to camp. François hurried ahead, intent on his moose horn and his gun. Barney Osborne, with a fishing line in his pocket, left the others and set out for a little pond he had discovered, where huge trout would come swirling after the salt pork on his hook. The rest of the men went down the path to the dam, and so across the river to the camp, loafing along in the joy of their week-end freedom.

That day not a trout would bite. Barney soon became discouraged, and started across the ridge through the woods to the river. In his hurry he swerved from the true direction, and instead of striking the river at the dam, came out at the dead water where the floating poplar lay. He started downstream. It was just at sunset, and the logs on the farther shore were tinted with old rose and gold. As he plunged ahead through the brush he came to a great birch tree that towered high above the low spruce and alders. On his left, by the water, was a little beach of coarse sand, against which floated poplar sticks in a thick mass. When Barney looked at the birch and the beach and the few lily pads growing up through the poplar a whimsical idea crept into his mind. He grinned, nodded and drew his knife. In ten minutes he held a long, conical horn, rudely made, but very much like the moose horn of François Latteau.

Barney put the horn to his lips, and moving it gently back and forth, uttered a wavering, long-drawn wail. It echoed from shore to shore, and died away in the evening stillness. Barney tried the call again and again, but no moose came. For twenty minutes he sat by the river, now calling, now waiting in silence. It was nearly dark. He gave a few grunts, holding the end of the horn close to the ground, and stirred a stick in the water, as he had seen François Latteau do; then in disgust he threw the rolled sheet of bark into the river.

As he got up and turned to look for his path his heart gave a great leap of fear; he stood transfixed with amazement and terror. Barney had brought no gun; he had been playing a game, and had not thought of a possible danger. But a beast had come out of the forest like a ghost in the night, as silently as September mist; with savage curiosity it scanned its summoner; red-eyed and sombre, it towered above him. There on the old road, with its mane bristling stiffly, with its antlers flung forward above its widespread forefeet and great tufted chin, stood the king of moose.

Barney raked his mind vainly for an avenue of escape. He could not have climbed the smooth-stemmed birch even if he could have reached it. Behind him lay the river jammed with poplar; beyond that was the camp and safety.

With a swinging shake of its mighty head the beast snorted, plunged forward, and stopped, striking its hoofs deep into the soft ground. Barney took a step toward the river. With a grunt of rage the bull started at him a second time, and Barney leaped from shore. To his ears came a bellow and a splash and many savage grunts. Barney ran with all his speed over the yielding sticks of poplar.

He was an old hand at river driving; he was as sure-footed as a cat, but the poplar had been cut where the growth was young, and the small logs sank under his weight, so that he had not taken a dozen steps before he was running ankle-deep in water. After he had made a hundred feet, his stride lagged; he slumped to his knees, and with the greatest difficulty raised his foot high enough for the next step. He jumped to a trunk large enough to support him, and once more caught his stride; but the shore was far ahead of him and dim in the deepening dusk. His heart was pounding and his lungs ached. Behind him he could hear the baffled moose raging. Barney knew that his one chance of escape lay in unremitting speed, for as surely as he lagged, the poplar would sink beneath him. He pressed doggedly on. As the minutes passed he grew dizzy with the exhausting effort. His foot missed a log, his leg shot hip-deep into the river, and he fell face down.

As he plunged downward he flung himself across the floating sticks, with his arms thrust out before him. The poplars kept him from sinking, but the icy water crept up round his body. He could rest from his terrific sprint, however, and holding his head high, he took in deep breaths of air. He heard no sound from either shore, and looking round, saw that his assailant had departed.

When Barney had recovered strength and breath he decided to go on, and taking hold of two poplars, started to get up. But the instant he shifted his weight to only two sticks they sank beneath him; his arms and knees went under, and his chin bumped hard on the other logs; he drew cold water into his nostrils, and for a moment he sputtered and coughed. The second time he chose his poplars more carefully, and held two in each hand. Priming every muscle for the start, he tried to spring to his feet and get away before the poplars should go under. But he fell again; this time he was entirely submerged. As he rose to the cold evening air he felt blood trickling from his bruised nose. He tried to hitch ahead to the shore little by little, but whenever he pushed one log back beneath him, he lost his balance, and his head went under water; and at best such progress was hopelessly slow.

The chill of the November twilight began to creep into his body; his teeth were chattering and his muscles felt numb. He was soaked from head to foot, and he gradually became aware that his clothes were freezing stiff on his back. A little fringe of ice was creeping out in swiftly forming crystals from the poplar stems. No man could live long in such exposure; in a frenzy of mad fear Barney strove unreasoningly, desperately, to regain his footing on the unstable logs. In his hopeless attempt he almost went entirely under the poplars, and with difficulty scrambled up again to his prostrate position across them.

It was very still on the river. Barney thought of the camp beyond the ridge, where the men were seated after supper, with the cook telling a long story and the "cookee" singing a Scotch song. He thought a little of the Miramichi and a log cabin by a deep spring, and then he began to feel warm and sleepy. The ice was creeping in round him, his clothes were stiffening. He looked at himself as if from a long way off, and he understood that he, the man lying on the river, was in great danger, but that there was a possibility of escape. Yes, he could escape!

With a start Barney woke from his dreaming. He concentrated all his will power and determination to banish the drowsy, comfortable, far-away feeling that made him think that it was time to sleep. Little by little he fought it off, biting his lips and splashing water into his face. When he had gained control of himself he went slowly to work.

He drew many poplars together, side by side, crawling partly over them as he pulled and hauled to make them even. Then with great difficulty he drew more poplars from the water and laid them across the others at right angles. Parallel with the first tier he laid yet another tier. The piled poplars stood inches up from the water. Another layer and another he laid, rolling them carefully together in even crisscross, and taking advantage of every knot, notch and branch to hold them together, for he had no rope to tie them. The raft stood a foot above the water. He was so very numb that he could hardly crawl up on the odd craft, but the effort of building it had saved him. As he climbed, very slowly, one poplar rolled off under his knee, and he rested for a minute without breathing. The raft held, and he lay above water. He raised himself to one knee, to one foot; he almost stood erect when suddenly a side of the raft sank inches under water; the logs tipped and tipped, and then in another moment the whole structure spread apart, and the carefully laid logs spilled in confusion.

Barney Osborne had thought that he could not move, that only to stand would take his last effort; but when he felt the raft lurch and go he made a wild leap. His feet struck a log, and he sprang forward in a lumbering, painful run. It was dark. Above him were small, cold stars and a crescent moon. Ahead, the wooded shores spread dim and low. Under him were deep black water and many poplar logs. He ran faster and faster, keeping his balance by instinct. As he stepped from the logs they made sucking, splashing sounds. His blood moved quickly and more quickly, and his feet, his hands, his legs and his arms tingled with fiery pains. His pumping lungs began to ache, but he never stopped; he ran on and on toward that dim shore line. He struggled on until he stumbled off the last poplar, fell into the water, and in despair let himself go down. But his feet touched the river bed; the water was only two feet deep! He floundered to the bank. Never stopping, he found the old tote road along the river, and broke into a slow jog trot that carried him over the ridge to camp.

He staggered into the cookroom with flushed face and pounding heart, and flung himself down by the hot stove; the men stared at him in amazement. Then from the yard came the sound of slow steps. François Latteau entered with his rifle and his moose horn, placed them very deliberately against the wall, and held his hands over the glowing stove covers.

"For two mortal hours have I hollered at that pond, and

never a sound did I hear," said François, scowling vindictively. "There ain't no such thing as a moose left in this country."

Barney Osborne, in the corner by the stove, burst into a great roar of laughter. Loud and long he laughed, while the men stood round in dumb amazement.

Once a Cowboy

Will James

It was a mean fall, and on that account the round-up wagons was late with the works, and later getting in at the winter quarters. The cold raw winds of the early mornings wasn't at all agreeable to get up in, and I'd just about got so I could choke the cook when he hollered "Come and get it, you rannies, before I throw it out." We'd hear that holler long before daybreak, and sticking our heads out from under our tarps we'd greet the new day with a cuss word and a snort.

A wet snow would be falling and laying heavy on our beds, and feeling around between the tarp and blankets for socks we'd took off wet the night before, we'd find 'em froze stiff, but by the time they was pulled on and made to fit again and the boots over 'em, buckled on chaps and all what we could find to keep a feller warm, we wasn't holding no grudge against the cook, we just wanted a lot of that strong steaming hot coffee he'd just made and had waiting for us.

The bunch of us would amble up and around the fire like a pack of wolves, only there was no growling done; instead there'd be remarks passed around such as, "This is what makes

a cowboy wonder what he done with his summer's wages."
There'd be a whoop and a holler and a bucking cowhand
would clatter up near top of the pots by the fire, "Make room,
you waddies, Ise frizzed from my brisket both ways," and slap-
ping his hands to his sides would edge in on the circle and grin
at the bunch there before him.

The lids of the big dutch ovens was lifted, steaks, spuds and
biscuits begin to disappear, but tracks was made most often
toward the big coffeepot, and when the bait is washed down
and the blood begins to circulate freer there was signs of daybreak, and rolling a cigarette we'd head for the muddy rope
corral.

Our ropes would be stiff as cables, and it was hard to make
a good catch. The particular pony you'd be wanting would
most generally stick his head in the ground like a ostrich, and
mixed in with about two hundred head of his kind and all a
milling around steady, he'd be mighty hard to find again in case
you missed your first throw.

Daylight being yet far off at that time, there's no way to
identify any of the ten or twelve horses in your string only by
the outline of their heads against the sky or by the white there
may be on their foreheads. You throwed your rope but you
couldn't see it sail and you didn't know you'd caught your
horse till you felt the rope tighten up, and sometimes when
you'd led out the horse you'd caught and got close to him it'd
be another horse — the one you'd throwed the rope at had
heard it coming and ducked.

Turning that horse back in the corral, you'd make another
loop and try to get another sight of the horse you wanted; when
you did, and the rope settled on him this time and let him out

— if he didn't have to be drug out by a saddle horse — to your saddle, then's when the fun most generally did begin.

The snow and sleet and cold wind made the ponies, young or old, mighty sensitive to whatever touched 'em; they'd kick, and buck, and strike then, no matter how gentle some of 'em might of been when the nice weather was on. The cowboy, all bundled up on account of the cold, his feet wet and in the slippery mud the wet snow had made, finds it all a big drawback in handling himself when saddling and a flying hoof comes.

The shivering pony don't at all welcome the frozen and stiff saddle blanket, and it might have to be put on the second time; getting a short hold and hanging on to the hackamore rope the cowboy then picks up the saddle and eases it on that pony's back, and before that pony can buck it off, a reach is made for the cinch, the latigo put through the cinch ring and drawed up. If you work fast enough and know how, all that can be done, and you don't have to pick up your saddle and blanket out of the mud.

I've seen it on many a morning of that kind and you'd just about have your pony half in the humor of being good, when some roman-nosed lantern-jawed bronc would go to acting up, jerk away from a rider and try to kick him at the same time and go to bucking and a bawling, and with an empty saddle on his back, hackamore rope a dragging, would make a circle of the rope corral where all the boys would be saddling up.

The ponies led out and shivering under the cold saddle that put a hump in their backs would just be a waiting for such an excuse as that loose hunk of tornado to start 'em, and with a loud snort and a buck half of 'em would jerk away. The cowboy had no chance holding 'em, for nine times out of ten that loose bronc would stampede past between him and the horse he was trying to hold, the hackamore rope would hook on the saddle of that bronc and it'd be jerked out of his hands.

Those folks who've seen rodeos from the grand stand most likely remember the last event of each day's doings; it's the wild-horse race, and maybe it'll be recollected how the track gets tore up by them wild ponies and how if one horse jerks loose he'll most likely make a few others break away. At them rodeos there's two men handling each horse, where with the round-up wagon on the range each man handles his horse alone.

And just picture for yourself the same happenings as you seen in the wild-horse race at the rodeo, only just add on to the picture that it's not near daylight, that instead of good sunshine and dry dirt to step on there's mud or gumbo six inches deep with snow and slush on top, the cowboy's cold wet feet, heavy wet chaps and coat that ties him down — a black cloudy sky, and with the cold raw wind comes a wet stinging snow to blind him.

That gives you a kind of an idea of how things may be along with the round-up wagon certain times of the year. Montana and Wyoming are real popular for rough weather as I've just described, and you can look for it there most every spring till late and sometimes in the fall starting early. I've seen that kind of weather last for two weeks at the time, clear up for one day and it was good to last for two weeks more.

It was no country for a tenderfoot to go playing cowboy in, besides the ponies of them countries wouldn't allow him to. It took nothing short of a long lean cowboy raised in the cow country to ride in it, and even though he'd cuss the weather, the country, and everything in general, there was a feeling back of them cuss words that brought a loving grin for the whole and the same that he was cussing.

Getting back to where a cowboy was saddling his horse and the stampeding bronc started the rumpus, I'll make it more natural and tell of how one little horse of that kind and on them cold mornings can just set the whole remuda saddled ponies and all to stampeding and leave near all the cowboys afoot.

Yessir, I remember well one cold drizzly morning that same fall, the wind was blowing at sixty per, the saddle blanket and saddle had to be put on at the same time or it'd blow out of the country. My horse was saddled and ready to top off, and pulling my hat down as far as I could get it I proceeds to do that. I'm getting a handful of mane along with a short holt on my reins and am just easing up in the saddle. When I gets up about half ways I meets up with the shadow of another horse trying to climb up on the other side of my horse. Me being only about a thousand pounds lighter than that shadow I'm knocked out of the way pronto, my horse goes down on part of me and that shadow keeps on a going as though there'd been nothing in its road.

That seemed to start things, and the wind that was blowing plenty strong already got a heap stronger, and all at once.

There was a racket of tearing canvas down by the chuck wagon and soon enough the big white tarpaulin that was covering that wagon breaks loose, comes a skipping over the brush, and then sails right up and amongst the two hundred saddle horses in the rope corral.

Them ponies sure didn't wait to see how and where it was going to light, they just picked up and flew, taking rope corral and everything right with 'em. A couple of the boys that was already mounted had to go too or else quit the pony they was riding, and they didn't have time to do that.

My horse being down for just the second he was knocked that way was up and gone, and I sure has to do some tall scrambling when the remuda broke out of the corral. I could near touch 'em as they went by and I'm drawing a long breath for the narrow escape I just had, when that same long breath is knocked out of me and I sails a ways, then lands in a heap. There must of been one horse I hadn't accounted for.

It's about daylight when I comes to enough to realize that I should pick myself up and get out of that brush I'd lit into. I'm gazing around kind of light-headed and wonders where everybody went, and finally, figgering that they'd be by the fire at the chuck wagon, makes my way that direction.

It's broad daylight by the time we hears the bells of the remuda coming back to the corral, some of the boys had put it up again while I was asleep in the brush, and the two riders what stampeded away when the remuda did was hazing the spooky ponies in again.

"Well, boys, we'll try it again," says the wagon boss as he dabs his rope on a big brown horse that was tearing around the corral.

Most of our ponies being already saddled it don't take us long to get lined out again. The boss is up on his horse, taking a silent count to see if any of his men are missing, while waiting for everybody to be on their horses and ready to follow him.

Our horses was all spooked up from that stampede, and when we started away from camp that morning it was a wild bunch for fair. I was trying to ease my pony into a lope without him breaking in two with me, and I just about had him out of the notion when there's a beller alongside of me, and I turns to see a bucking streak of horseflesh with a scratching cowboy atop of it headed straight my way.

It's a good thing I was ready to ride, 'cause my horse had been aching to act up from the start, and that example headed our way more than agreed with his spirits at that time. He went from there and started to wipe up the earth, and every time he'd hit the ground he'd beller, "I'll get you!"

At first I was satisfied to just be able to keep my saddle under me, but come a time when as my blood started circulating and getting warmed up on the subject that my spirits also answered the call and agreed with the goings on; then's when I begins to reefing him, and my own special war whoop sure tallied up with the bellering of that active volcano under me.

A glance to one side, and I notice that I'm not the only one who's putting up a ride, the rain and snow mixed kept me from seeing very far, but I could see far enough to tell that at least half the riders was busy on the same engagement that drawed my attention just then; one of the ponies had took a dislike for the cook and, tearing up everything as he went, was chasing him over pots and pans and finally under the wagon. The cowboy on top of that bronc was near losing his seat for laughing; he'd never seen the cook move that fast before.

We're out of camp a couple of miles before the usual rumpus quiets down, and stringing out on a high lope we all heads for a high point we don't see but know of, and some ten miles away. From that point the boss scatters the riders, and in pairs we branch out to circle and comb the country on the way back, running all the stock we see to the cutting grounds.

I'm riding along, trying to look through the steady-falling

drizzle snow for stock; it seemed to me that I was born and raised under a slicker, on a wet saddle, riding a kinky bronc, going through slush and snow, and facing cold winds. It struck me as a coon's age since I seen good old sunshine, and for the first time I begins to wonder if a cow-puncher ain't just a plain locoed critter for sticking along with the round-up wagons as he does; it's most all knocks, and starting from his pony's hoofs on up to the long sharp horns of the ornery critters he's handling, along with the varieties the universe hands him in weather — twelve to sixteen hours in the saddle, three to four changes of horses a day, covering from seventy-five to a hundred miles, then there's one to two hours night guard to break the only few hours left to get rest in.

We was moving camp for the last time that year, the next stop was the home ranch, and when we hooked up the cook's six-horse team and handed him the ribbons we all let out a war whoop that started the team that direction on a high lope. The cook wasn't holding 'em back any, and hitting it down a draw to the river bottoms the flying chuck wagon swayed out of sight.

Us riders was bringing in upwards of a thousand head of weaners and we didn't reach the big fields till late that day, when we finally got sight of the big cottonwoods near hiding the long log building of the home ranch; that, along with the high pole corrals, the sheds and stables, all looked mighty good to me again.

The stock turned loose, we all amble towards the corrals to unsaddle; I tries to lead my horse in the dry stable, but him being suspicious of anything with a roof on won't have it that way. "All right, little horse," I says to him, "if you're happier to be out like you've always been used to, I'm not going to try to spoil you," and pulling off my wet saddle I hangs it where it's dry for once. The pony trots off a ways, takes a good roll and, shaking himself afterwards, lets out a nicker and lopes out to join the remuda.

"Just like us punchers," I remarks, watching him; "don't know no better."

Over eight months had passed since I'd opened a door and set my feet on a wooden floor, and when I walks in the bunk house and at one end sees a big long table loaded down with hot victuals, and chairs to set on, I don't feel at all natural, but I'm mighty pleased at the change.

The ranch cook is packing in more platters, and watching him making tracks around the table, looking comfortable and not at all worried of what it may be like outside, I'll be daggone if I didn't catch myself wishing I was in his warm moccasins.

The meal over with, I drags a bench over by one of the windows and, listening some to the boys what was going over the events that happened on the range that summer, I finds myself getting a lot of satisfaction from just a-setting there and looking out of the window; it was great to see bum weather and still feel warm and comfortable. I gets to star-gazing and thinking, so that I plum forgets that there's twenty cowboys carrying on a lot of conversation in the same big room.

I'd just about come to the conclusion I was through punching cows when one of the boys digs me in the ribs and hollers, "Wake up, Bill! Time for second guard."

I did wake up, and them familiar words I'd heard every night for the last eight months struck me right where I lived;

they was said as a joke, but right there and then I was sure I'd never want to stand no more of them midnight guards.

The work was over, and all but a few of the old hands was through. The superintendent gave us to understand as a parting word that any or all of us are welcome to stay at the ranch and make ourselves to home for the winter. "You can keep your private saddle horses in the barn and feed 'em hay. The cow foreman tells me," he goes on, "that you've all been mighty good cowboys, and I'm with him in hoping to see you all back with the outfit in time for the spring works."

A couple of days later finds me in town, my own top horse in the livery stable and me in a hotel. I makes a start to be anything but a cowboy by buying me a suit, a cap, shoes, and the whole outfit that goes with the town man. I then visits the barber and the bathtub, and in an hour I steps out thinking that outside my complexion and the way I walks I looks about the same as everybody else I see on the street.

I takes it easy for a few days, then gradually I tries to break myself to looking for a job where there's no ponies or bellering critters to contend with. I wanted an inside job where the howling blizzard wouldn't reach me and where I could have a roof over my head at night instead of a tarpaulin.

Time goes on, and it seems like my education is lacking considerable to qualify for the job I set out to get; you had to know as much as a schoolma'am to even get a look in. I made a circle every day and run in all the likely places I'd see.

I'm some leg weary as I makes my way back to the hotel one night, and going to my room I stretches out on the bed to rest up a little before I go out to eat. I have a feeling that all ain't well with me as I lays there thinking.

I don't want to think that I'm hankering to get back to the range, so blames it to the new ways of everything in general what comes with town life, and I tries to cheer myself up with the idea that I'll soon get used to it and in time like it.

"I got to like it," I says to myself, "and I'm going to stay with it till I do, 'cause I'm through with punching cows"; and getting up real determined I goes out to hunt a restaurant.

I'd been feeding up on ham and eggs and hamburger steak with onions ever since I hit town, and this night I thought I'd change my order to something more natural and what I'd been used to on the range.

"Bring me a rib steak about an inch thick," I says to the waiter. "Don't cook it too much, but just cripple the critter and drag 'er in."

I kept a waiting for the order to come, and about concluded he must of had to wait for the calf to grow some, when here he comes finally. I tackles the bait on the platter, and I was surprised to see a piece so much like beef, and still taste so different from any I'd ever et before. With a lot of work I managed to get away with half of it, and then my appetite, game as it was, had to leave me.

The waiter comes up smiling as he sees I'm about through, and hands me the bill. "I don't want to spread it around," I says as I picks up the bill and goes to leave, "but between you and me, I'll bet you that steak you brought me has been cooked in the same grease that's been cooking my ham and eggs these last two weeks. I can taste 'em."

The weather had been good and stayed clear ever since I hit town, but as I walks out of the restaurant I notice a breeze had sprung up, and snow was starting to fall. I finds myself taking long whiffs of air that was sure refreshing after stepping out of that grub-smelling emporium.

Feeling rested up some, I faces the breeze for a walk and to no place in particular. I'm walking along, thinking as I go, when looking around to get the lay of my whereabouts I notices that right across the street from where I'm standing is the livery stable where I'd left my horse, and being that I'd only been over to see him once since I'd rode in, thinks I'd enjoy the feel of his hide once more.

The stable man walks in on us as we're getting real sociable, and with a "Howdy" asks if I may be looking for a job. "Man named Whitney, got a ranch down the river about fifty miles, asked me to look out for a man who'd want a job breaking horses on contract, and I thought maybe you'd be wanting to take it."

"Not me," I says, feeling tempted and refusing before considering. "I'm not riding any more, and I been looking for work in town."

"Did you try the Hay and Grain Market next block up the street?" he asks. "They was looking for a man some time back."

No, I hadn't tried it, but the next day bright and early I was on the grounds and looking for the major-domo of that outfit.

At noon that day I'd changed my suit, and putting on a suit of Mexican serge I went to work. My job was clerking, and on the retail end of the business, filling in orders and help load the stuff on the wagon of the customers.

And that night, when the place closed up and I walks to my hotel I felt a heap better than any time since I'd hit town. Of course I wasn't in love with the job, it was quite a change and mighty tame compared to punching cows, but then I figgered a feller had to allow some so's to get what he's after.

I gets along fine with everybody around, and it ain't long before I'm invited to different gatherings that's pulled off now and again. I gets acquainted more as I stays on, and comes a time when if feeling sort of lonesome I know where to go and spend my evenings.

I'd manage to stop in at the stable and say "Hello" to my gray horse most every night when the work was through, and with everything in general going smooth I thought it wasn't so bad.

There was times though when coming to my room I'd find myself staring at my chaps and boots with the spurs still on and where I'd put 'em in the corner. They got to drawing my attention so that I had to hide 'em in the closet where I couldn't see 'em, and then I thinks, "What about my horse and saddle? A town man don't have no need for anything like that."

But somehow I didn't want to think on that subject none at all right then, and I drops it, allowing that a feller can't break away from what all he's been raised with or at in too short a time.

That winter was a mean one, just as mean as the fall before, I still remembered; the snow was piled up heavy on the hills around town and every once in a while there'd be another storm adding on a few inches. The sight of it and the cold winds a howling by on the streets kept me contented some, and it all helped break me in to the new ways of living I'd picked on.

I'd been on the job a month or so when I notice that my

appetite begins to leave me. I changes eating places often, but they all seemed to have the same smell as you walked in, and there was times when I felt like taking the decorated platter and all outside and eating it there.

And what's more, my complexion was getting light, too light.

January and February had come and went, the cold spell broke up some, and then March set in wild and wicked. I'm still at my job at the Feed Market and my wages being raised once along with promises of another raise soon, proves that I'm doing well. What's more, my time had been took up considerable on account of me meeting up with a young lady what put my gray horse a far second in my thoughts, and when I'd walk past the stable I'd most generally be in too big a hurry to stop and see him. One day the stable man stops me as I'm hurrying by and tells me that he has a chance to sell that little horse for me for a hundred dollars.

That was a call for a show-down to myself, and of a sudden I realized that parting with that horse I was parting with the big open range I'd been born and raised into. I studies it over for quite a spell and finds the more I thinks the more my heart lays the ways of where that horse can take me, and my mind all a milling I can't decide.

I walks away, telling the stable man I'd let him know later.

I does a lot of comparing between the range and the town, and finds that both has qualities and drawbacks, only in town it was easier living, maybe too easy, but I figgered that here was more of a future.

Just the other day I was told by the main owner at the market that they was figgering on quitting the business and retiring, and that there'd be a good opportunity for a serious-thinking man like myself to grab. It was suggested that I could let my wages ride and buy shares with 'em as I worked till there'd come a time as I kept at it when I'd find myself part owner of a good business and a steady income.

That night I went to see the young lady, who by this time had a lot to say as to my actions. I didn't let her know what was going on in my think tank, 'cause I wanted to fight it out by myself; besides I'd come to conclusions, and long before I left her to go back to my hotel.

The next morning I stops by and tells the stable man that if he can get a hundred dollars for that little horse of mine, to take it. But it hit me pretty hard and I didn't go by the stable any more after that, not for a long time.

April come, and with the warm weather that came with it the snow started to melting, the streets was muddy, and the gutters was running full; it was spring, and even with all the resolutions I'd made, I didn't feel any too strong right then.

I was afraid to give my imagination full swing and think of the home ranch on the Big Dry; I knew the boys that came back for the spring works would be out on the horse round-up and getting ready to pull out with the wagons.

Each cowboy would be topping off his string about now, the bronc peeler would be picking out a bunch of green colts from the stock horses and start in breaking, the cook would be a cleaning up the chuck box on the back end of that wagon, and the cow foreman, glancing often on the road that leads from town to the ranch, would be looking for any of the missing cowboys what was with him the year before.

I found it mighty hard to walk away from that spring sun-shine into the building where I was working. There was orders on the desk waiting for me to fill, and picking 'em up I walks among high walls of grain and baled hay.

Everybody I'd see would remark how great it was outside in the spring air, and rubbing their hands would get to work at the desk and typewriter, and forget all about it the minute they set down.

I felt sorry for 'em in a way, 'cause it struck me as though they'd never had a chance to really appreciate springtime — or was it that their years in captivity that way had learnt 'em better than to hanker for such?

Anyway, I sure didn't seem to be able to dodge how I felt. My girl and everybody else noticed it, and even though I'd try to laugh it off I'd soon find myself picturing little white-faced calves scattered out either playing or sunning themselves while their mammies was feeding on the new green grass.

I could near feel the slick shiny hide of the ponies after their long winter hair had just fell off. And dag-gone it, it was getting the best of me.

I'd catch myself sneaking glances at the green hills around the town and feeling as though I had no right to. And once in a while in the evening as I'd be walking to my room and I'd hear a meadow lark a-singing way off in the distance, I'd look at the buildings, the sidewalks and streets as though they was a scab on this earth. I wanted my horse under me and lope out away from it.

I'd done a heap of reasoning with myself, and kept a pointing out all the whys I should forget the range and get used to the town, and I'd pretty near give in as long as I was in my room and couldn't feel the breeze, but once outside again and a meadow lark sang out, my heart would choke out all what the town offered and leave breath only for the blue ridges and the big stretches that layed past 'em.

Then came a day when my hide got too thick to feel the reasoning spur I was giving it. Something way deep inside of me took charge of things and I finds myself making tracks towards the stable.

I sneaks in, and I had to rub my eyes considerable to make sure that there in the same box stall was my little gray horse, fat as a seal and a snorting like a steam engine.

"Dag-gone your hide!" I says, and I makes a grab for him, he's pawing the air snorting and a-rearing, but I'm hanging on to his neck with a death grip and hands him all the pet cuss words I can think of.

The stable man runs up to see what's making all the rumpus, and his expressions tell me plain he thinks I'm drunk and celebrating. I was drunk all right, but not on the same stuff that's handed over the bar.

"Sorry I couldn't sell him for you," I hear him say as I let go of my horse and walks up to him, "but the fellow what wanted him came over one day to try the horse out and the little son of a gun throwed him off as fast as he'd get on; he brought another feller over the next day and the same thing happened. Too bad he acts that way," he goes on, " 'cause he's a right pretty horse."

"You're dag-gone right he's a pretty horse," I says; "the prettiest horse I ever seen."

It's three days later when I gets sight of the Triangle F main herd, then the remuda, and down in a creek bottom by a bunch of willows is the chuck wagon.

There's war whoops from the bunch as I lopes into sight, and the wagon boss comes up to meet me. "I knowed you'd be back, Bill," he says, smiling, "and I got your string of ponies a waiting for you, twelve of 'em."

And on guard that night, riding around the bedded herd, I was singing a song of the trail herd, happy again, and just a cowboy.

The Familiar Path

Lois Lenski

"*Ach*, don't pull so!" cried Suzanna.

"Stand still, once," said her older sister. "Stop wiggling."

The big kitchen was a busy place. The children were getting up. It was still dark outside, so the lamp over the table was lit.

Bib and Beck, the two big girls, whose real names were Barbara and Rebecca, were already dressed. Beck and the boys had gone outside with their father and mother to milk the cows. The twins sat half dressed on the floor playing. Henry, five, snatched his hat and ran out too. Sammy, three, still in bed, began to cry.

Bib dipped the comb into the basin. She parted Suzanna's hair and began to wet it. She made neat twists over each ear and pulled them back.

"Not so tight! Not so tight!" cried Suzanna.

Bib made two long braids in back, coiled them in a knot and pinned it with hairpins.

"There now, Susie," she said. "You're done."

"Why do you make it so fierce tight?" asked Suzanna. "I can't even turn my head! It hurts terrible!"

But Bib paid no attention. "Who's next? Punkin or Puddin?"

The twins, age seven, looked just alike. They had the same blue eyes, the same brown hair, the same pointed chins and fat cheeks. They were the same height too. Their real names, Anna and Ada, were seldom used. When they were fat babies, Uncle Dave had called them Punkin and Puddin, and the names had stuck. The Fishers loved nicknames.

Bib, who was fourteen, had plenty to do. She was frying mush for breakfast, trying to comb the twins' hair and pack the school lunches all at once.

"Put in a piece of shoo-fly pie for me," said Suzanna.

"*Ach* now, all you want is shoo-fly pie," said Bib. "We've only got one and it's not enough for breakfast. Here, put it on the table. I'll bake some more today after school and you can help me."

She handed a large pie with a crumby top to her sister.

"Punkin and Puddin, get the table set," called Bib. "Hurry a little or we'll all be late for school."

The little girls took knives, forks and plates to the long table by the window. They hopped up and down on the long benches. They were very light on their bare feet. They set eleven places — there were nine children and Dat and Mam.

It was getting light now and the others came in. Mam put out the light in the gas lamp as the morning sun streamed in through the east window. Then she brought Sammy from his bed. Everybody washed at the basin and sat down.

All but Suzanna. She was not there. They never started a meal until all were there.

"Where's that girl?" asked Mam. "Beck, Bib, where is she?"

"*Susie! Susie!*" Bib called.

The door of the kettle house opened and Suzanna came running. She slid into place on the girls' bench.

"Move over!" she said, licking her lips. "Gimme room, Punkin."

"Silence!" said Dat. "Hands on laps. Fold your hands."

They bowed their heads. Mam and Dat moved their lips and prayed silently, eyes closed. The children prayed too, without a sound. Then they reached for food and ate. They spread pork pudding on fried mush and ate it. They had "coffee soup" — coffee poured over bread cubes. All but Suzanna, who licked her lips again. She was not hungry. She hoped no one would notice.

"Clean your plates," said Dat.

Nobody talked. They were too hungry, too busy eating.

Suzanna slid her slice of mush onto Reuben's plate. He wolfed it down. Nobody saw.

"Heck! No pie this morning?" cried Jonas.

Jonas was the oldest, fifteen. He liked to think himself a man, just because he was through school. He had finished the eighth grade and did not have to go any more.

"Who's hiding the shoo-fly pie this morning?" asked Dat. Breakfast was not breakfast without it.

"Why, Suzanna!" said Bib. "I gave it to you to put on the table." She looked but there was no pie in sight. "What did you do with it?"

Suzanna jumped up, ready to be off. Then she knew there was no escape. She must stay at table until everyone had finished eating and they had prayed again. She sat down.

Mam repeated the question. "What did you do with the pie, Susie?"

Suzanna hesitated. Then she wailed, "Do we have to have pie *every* day for breakfast?"

"That's not the point," said Mam. "*What did you do with it?*"

Suzanna hung he head. They were all looking at her now. "I hid it."

"Hid it? Where?" asked Mam.

"In the kettle house," said Suzanna.

"Go get it then," said Mam. "Why on earth did you hide it?"

Oh dear, Mam always had to know everything. "Because . . . because . . . I dropped it!" said Suzanna.

She might as well tell it all. There could never be any secrets in this house. "I *dropped* it and *smashed* it . . . and then . . . and then . . ." She might as well confess. "It wasn't any good for anything . . . so I picked it up . . . and . . ."

"Then what?" asked Dat. He spoke in a gentle voice, not scolding at all.

"*Then I just ate it up!*"

The words sounded frightening in the silence. Suzanna looked at Mam, lips set tight and black frown getting blacker. She was in for it now. She'd get a terrible licking. Eating a whole pie! Who ever heard of such a thing?

But thunder and lightning did not strike.

Out of the silence came a cackle of laughter.

It was Rags, Reuben by name, whose laugh was like a hen cackling. Then Dat began to roar and all the others joined in. Suzanna looked up and saw a broad smile on her mother's face. She was safe — no yardstick this time!

"So that's why you weren't hungry for breakfast!" said Mam. "You were full of shoo-fly pie!"

They laughed and laughed. Would they never get done laughing? What was so funny about eating pie? No licking, thought Suzanna, but this might be worse. They would tease her to death.

"Hi, Shoo-Fly!" cried Jonas, the biggest tease of all. "Been shooin' any flies lately?"

"She's got her tummy full of shoo-fly," cried Rags.

They pointed their fingers and Susie wept.

She had earned a permanent nickname. From this time on her name was seldom Suzanna or even Susie. It was Shoo-Fly.

Bib did not forget. Bib never forgot anything. That day after school, she saw to it that Suzanna made a shoo-fly pie, her first. It was Friday, baking day. Mam had been baking bread all day long in the big oven in the kettle house. Bib had to bake the cakes and pies. They were getting ready for Saturday. They would sell them at the pie stand on the highway.

Suzanna Fisher, formerly called Susie and now Shoo-Fly, was a little Amish girl. She lived on a farm in Lancaster County, Pennsylvania. Her parents, grandparents and all her ancestors had been Amish since they came to America from Switzerland in the early 1700s. They were a strict religious sect who lived as close to the teachings of the Bible as they knew how. They kept themselves apart from the world and its ways. They had a way of life all their own. The Amish children were used to hard work. As soon as they could walk, they had chores of their own to do.

Suzanna had made *schnitz* or dried apple pies before. They were easy. A shoo-fly pie was different and took longer. Bib told her just how to do it. How to mix brown sugar, flour and butter to make the crumbs. How to mix molasses with hot

105

water and soda and pour it in a pastry shell. Then put the crumby mixture on top and bake it.

"Why do they call it *shoo-fly* pie?" asked Suzanna.

Bib shook her head. "Don't ask me!" she said. Bib was always serious. "That's its name. We've always called it that."

It was the same answer Suzanna always got. Why do we wear black bonnets? We've always done so. Why do we wear black aprons? We've always done so. Why do we have church in a house and not in a church? Why do we do things this way? We've always done it this way. Our grandparents and great-grandparents did it this way. So we do it too. We are Amish. We do not change. Suzanna had heard it over and over. She would hear it all her life. She would say it to her children.

"But *why* do they call it shoo-fly pie?" she asked again. "*I* know. Because it's so good, the flies like it — and you have to shoo them away."

Bib looked at her smiling.

"You ought to know how good it is," she said. "You ate a whole pie."

On Saturday, Bib had to stay home and do the Saturday cleaning. Besides, Bib liked housework and Beck didn't. So Beck hitched the horse Skipper to the carriage and packed the bread, cakes and pies in the back. Mam told Suzanna she could go along. But she did not want to go.

"I want to stay here," she said. "I want to see Grossmama and Aunt Suzanna . . . I want to help them . . . They need me . . . ."

She tried to think up excuses, but the truth was she did not like to go away at all. Out on the highway where all the cars were, she was frightened. She was scared of strangers too. No telling what they might do or say. It was bad enough to have to go to school. Home was the best place, the safest place to be.

But Suzanna had to obey. Like every Amish child, she had to obey without question. She put on her long purple school dress and black apron, she tied her purple bonnet under her chin. She heard her mother talking to Rebecca. Talking about *her*.

"It will soon be Suzanna's turn. She is old enough, she can make change. She can do the selling from now on, once she learns how."

Make change! Do the selling! Talk to strangers? Was Mam crazy? What was she thinking of?

"Get a move on, Shoo-Fly. Mam's waiting!" called Rags outside holding the horse.

Suzanna climbed into the buggy. She sat down in the back next to the boxes of baked goods. She was hemmed in by the darkness. She could not see a thing. The buggy had covered top and sides, and the curtain was down at the back. It was like a little house. There was one little window to peek out of. It was a good place to hide. It would be a good place to lie down and sleep — if they'd only let her.

Skipper's hoofs made a steady *clop-clopping* down the lane and out on the road. The buggy wheels squeaked and crunched on the loose gravel. Mam and Beck talked in low voices. After a while they made a turn and started again on the paved road. Soon a loud roar like that of a lion was heard, and a big automobile came bearing down on them. Suzanna could hear it, even if she could not see it. It was a big monster going to eat them . . . . She held her breath. But it went on by and left her to her dreams. Other cars came and went but she did not notice them.

All too soon they came to a stop. Everybody piled out at the pie stand. It was like a little table with a roof on top. Dat and Uncle Chris had made it. Beck unhitched Skipper and backed the buggy up behind. She and Mam took the baked goods and vegetables out. Also jars of Mam's apple and pear butter, cherry and plum jam. They set them on the stand. Beck fixed them to look nice. She and Mam talked about prices.

Cars began to stop. The people in them were not Amish. They did not speak Dutch, so the Amish people called them "English"— because they all spoke English. Suzanna spoke English too — at school. She could read and write and spell it. But at home she spoke in Dutch. These people who spoke English all the time were queer. They wore fancy clothes in gay patterns and bright colors. When Suzanna asked about it, her mother said, "They are not like us. We are the plain people. We are Amish." The same answer over and over again.

Each time a car stopped, Suzanna hid. Sometimes she climbed in "her house" in the buggy. Sometimes she had only time to duck under the counter, so people would not see her. Mam had to explain, "She's terrible bashful — this one."

When they were alone, Mam told her, "You must learn how to sell the pie and cake."

"*Ach,* no!" The thought terrified her. "I can't!"

Mam told her the prices. "Cake $1.25, corn 50¢ a dozen, bread 25¢, pie 85¢." Suzanna repeated the prices after her. She looked at Beck's black pocketbook on a long shoulder strap. It might be fun to wear it. It might be fun, after all, to jingle the coins and make change. . . .

"Stand here," said Mam. "Don't you go hide. You might as well get used to strangers. They won't bite you. Stand here and shoo the flies away." She gave her a piece of paper.

Just then a man came up. He got out of the largest black car Suzanna had ever seen. The man had no beard and wore no hat. How funny he looked! He was fat and had a gold pin in his bright red tie. He had a big cigar in his mouth and kept puffing. Mam was fixing things in the buggy. She turned her back to him.

For an Amish girl, Beck was very bold. Mam had told her how to talk to tourists. "Where are you from, Mister?" she asked.

"Massachusetts," the man said.

"You're a long ways from home," said Beck. That was what you said to all of them.

The man looked at Beck. He saw her bonnet and cape and apron.

"You're Amish," he said. "What's your name?"

"Rebecca Fisher," said Beck in a low voice. "What's yours?"

"I'm not telling," said the man.

Then he saw Suzanna shooing the flies away.

"What's *your* name?" he asked.

Suzanna ducked behind Beck and did not answer.

"Cat's got your tongue!" teased the man.

Suzanna peeked around and stuck out her tongue at him. There! That would stop him. Why should he know her name? He was a stranger.

"*Ach,* Susie!" scolded Beck under her breath. "Don't act so. He won't buy anything!"

"You don't need to tell me your name," said the man. "I

know it already. You're *Shoo-Fly Girl,* because you shoo the flies away."

How did *he* know? Could he read people's minds? Did he know she ate a whole shoo-fly pie just yesterday? How did he ever guess her nickname?

"Shoo-Fly Girl!" said the man again.

Beck laughed. Mam heard and laughed too. Suzanna hated him. She'd never be Suzanna or Susie any more. She'd always be Shoo-Fly.

"Shoo-Fly made the shoo-fly pie!" Beck lifted it up. "That's for sure!"

"She did?" he said. "That little thing? No bigger than a minute? Can she bake pies? I'll take it."

He paid the money, took the pie and went back to his car.

After they were sold out, Mam and Beck and Shoo-Fly drove home again. Everything looked just the same, the big "bank" barn, the windmill, the double house, the four big martin boxes on tall poles in the barnyard. Why couldn't the martins stay longer? Suzanna liked to watch them swoop across the sky and come back down to their houses. She looked at her own house — the house so plain, no curtains, with green shades pulled down halfway, neat and clean, the house called home.

It was noon and Bib had dinner ready. After dinner, Shoo-Fly skipped out. Saturday, no school, a time to be free and do as you please. Mam had sewing to do — that would keep her indoors. The sewing for nine children, making all their clothes, was never done. Bib and Beck put on their oldest clothes and went out to the tobacco field.

"I don't want to work, do you?" said Shoo-Fly to Rags.

"No," said Rags, "but we'll have to."

He had his raggediest clothes on, ready for whatever might come. He did not have as many ideas for escaping work as Shoo-Fly did.

"I'll tell you what," said Shoo-Fly. "We'll rub our arms with poison ivy, then we won't have to help."

"O.K.," said Rags. He cackled with glee. "Where will we find some?"

Shoo-Fly led the way to a shady place down by the creek. She picked bunches of three-pointed leaves, crushed them between stones and rubbed the paste on Rags's arms and her own. It colored them nice and green. She rubbed it on their bare legs and feet too.

"Now we're safe," she said.

"But won't it hurt?" asked Rags. "I had it once and it itched me terrible."

"It goes away soon," said Shoo-Fly. "Now we can go out and watch the others work."

Shoo-Fly liked to be out where the others were. She did not want to miss anything. It was a wonderful September day, crisp and cool, but sunny. She went tearing across to the tobacco field. She was so thin and her feet were so light, they hardly touched the ground. Rags came too, but more slowly. He liked to take his time. Then came Henry and Sammy and behind them, Pretzel, barking loudly. Pretzel, a nondescript dog, got his name because he liked to eat pretzels.

Henry, only five, was not called Hayfork for nothing. He could handle a man's hayfork like a man. His blond bobbed hair made a halo around his smiling face under the broad brim of his black felt hat. He always wore his hat outdoors.

The children ran to the field and stopped.

The tobacco had been cut and the men were working at the far end of the five-acre field. Dat was not a farmer like Uncle Chris. He had a carriage shop and Uncle Chris farmed the farm. But today Dat was out helping. Beck and Bib were helping too. The tobacco had to be cut and hung up in the shed and barn to dry before frost.

Everybody was working fast. The stalks that stood so strong and tall now lay on the ground. The workers speared them, five stalks to a lath. The girls wore old gray aprons up to their necks. They had red kerchiefs tied over their hair.

"We'd better not go too close," said Rags.

"Hi, you kids, come over here and get to work!" called Bib.

"I told you so," said Rags.

Bib called again. They went up closer, but not too close.

"We can't work," said Shoo-Fly. "We've got poison ivy. Our arms and legs are sore. They itch terrible!" She showed Bib her arms, but Bib just laughed.

"Another one of your tricks," she said, but she let them alone.

"Let's go play on the wagon," said Hayfork.

They climbed on the tobacco wagon and helped little Sammy up. They jumped down from the wagon and climbed up again. They jumped up and down. It was fun. Pretzel barked madly.

Then Beck called. "Come here, Shoo-Fly, and get to work. We are loading now and you can help."

Dat came up and said, "Come, girl, we need all the help we can get."

"I told you so," said Rags.

Poison ivy or no poison ivy, Shoo-Fly had to obey. She picked up a lath and speared five tobacco plants on it. The loaded lath was heavy, but she lifted it up to the wagon. Hayfork helped her. "I'm as strong as a man!" he bragged.

Then he and Shoo-Fly began to load the girls' laths on the wagon. It made good teamwork. But they soon grew tired. Shoo-Fly whispered in Hayfork's ear. They had worked long enough. His smile beamed approval. The next minute they both jumped down from the wagon and went running across the field. Sammy tagged behind. Rags kept right on working.

"Let's go to the carriage shop," said Shoo-Fly.

Hayfork nodded. "And see Jonas," he said.

Uncle Chris was Dat's brother. He and Aunt Emma lived out by the road, near the carriage shop. Their children were still babies. Dat made and repaired Amish carriages and buggies. Jonas helped in the shop or on the farm wherever needed. The shop was always full of all kinds of buggies, old, new, broken down or half finished. It was a good place to play.

Jonas was there today mixing paint. Dat's helper, old Ephraim Esh, was inside working at the forge.

"*Ach,* see Cousin Eli's pony cart!" cried Shoo-Fly.

Hayfork and Shoo-Fly stared. The new cart stood outside in the sun. It was beautiful — shiny black with red trim. It had lamps on the sides, electric, fed from batteries under the seat. Jonas came out and showed them everything.

"It's just finished," he said. "Watch out for wet paint!"

"*Ach,* Jonas!" cried Shoo-Fly. "Such a cart for . . ."

"Too good for that little spoiled brat, Eli," said Jonas.

"Eli gets what he wants," said Hayfork. At five, Henry was wise beyond his years.

Eli was their cousin, Uncle Dave's older son. Eli had a brown and white pony called Buster. Now Eli was getting a new pony cart. Uncle Dave had ordered it from Dat.

"Give us a ride in it, Jonas!" begged Hayfork, starting to pick up the shafts. "Be a pony and pull us."

"Drop it!" cried Jonas. "The paint's not dry."

Hayfork jumped back.

Across the road from Uncle Chris's house and the shop stood another farmhouse. A large truck pulled out of its lane and went rattling down the road. The house had been empty for some time.

"New people just moved in," said Jonas, looking up.

"Somebody we know?" asked Shoo-Fly.

"No," said Jonas. "They're 'English.' "

"Oh!" said Shoo-Fly, disappointed. She saw the door open and several children come out. "There's a girl," she said.

"There's a boy about my age and some little ones," said Jonas.

"Where they from?" asked Shoo-Fly.

"I don't know," said Jonas.

The new children were curious. They came out their lane and walked along the road. They came closer and closer to the carriage shop, as if half afraid. They came as close as they dared. They did not speak.

Shoo-Fly and her brothers watched them come. The girl was about Shoo-Fly's age, ten or so, the others younger. They looked at the pony cart. They looked at Shoo-Fly and her brothers. Jonas and Hayfork and Shoo-Fly began to talk in Pennsylvania Dutch.

Then the girl spoke. "What's that lingo you're speaking?

What are you talking about?" She could not understand Dutch.

No one answered. She turned to her little sister and said, "Listen to their funny talk!"

Her little brother had darted into the shop.

"Where's my brother?" the girl called. "Where's Robert?"

Shoo-Fly flew with her into the shop.

There was Robert with little Sammy. They had found an open can of black grease. They had smeared it all over their faces and clothes. They were black and sticky from head to foot.

"Oh! Oh!" cried the girl. "Look at Robert!"

Shoo-Fly knew just what to do. She found some lava soap that Dat and Jonas used. She washed the grease off the boys' hands and faces. But she could not get it off their clothes.

The strange girl took her brother and sister and went home. She did not say anything.

"They're mad at us," said Shoo-Fly.

"Who cares?" laughed Jonas.

It was on the way home that Jonas found the crow. A flock of crows was circling around a tree, cawing loudly. Then they took wing and darted low across the field. The boys began throwing stones at them. Suddenly one dropped to the ground.

"*Ach,* you killed it!" cried Shoo-Fly.

Hayfork picked the crow up and gave it to Jonas.

"Is it dead, Jonas?" asked Shoo-Fly.

"No," said Jonas, "only stunned. It's not hurt at all. There's not a drop of blood."

"There! It's opening its eyes," said Shoo-Fly. "It's alive."

"It's a young crow, about half grown," said Jonas.

"Give it to me," said the girl.

Jonas and Hayfork went running ahead across the field. Shoo-Fly cuddled the crow in her apron.

"I'll tame it," she said. "I'll have a pet all my own."

She walked slowly and the world was filled with the song of birds, the smell of the good earth and the warm glow of the setting sun.

◆ ◆ ◆

Nobody liked the crow but Shoo-Fly. The more the others hated it, the more she loved it.

That first day she fed it bread and milk. She spooned food and water into its bill. She made a straw bed in a little chicken pen for it. The front was made of wire, so the bird could not get out. Each day the crow grew stronger. Soon it began to know her and to make noises.

When she let it out, the little boys and the twins teased it and chased it. Punkin pulled a feather out and the crow pecked her. Puddin squeezed it hard and it bit her. So they soon learned to let it alone.

Shoo-Fly took it out each day and put it back in its pen at night. It was a great comfort to her. It was wonderful to have something that nobody else wanted. This was an important thing to learn in a large family.

Now Jonas had something new to tease her about. Whenever he saw the crow, he shouted, "Hi, Shoo-Fly! Come shoo this old black thief away!"

Shoo-Fly teased Jonas too. "What's that black fuzz on your chin, Jonas? Are you growing a beard, so you can go courting?"

But Jonas always had an answer. "When I grow up," he said, "I'm going to wear neckties and buttons, cut my hair short and shave off my beard!"

It was a daring threat and Shoo-Fly was shocked. Amish men did not wear neckties and had hooks and eyes on their outer clothes in place of buttons. They all had beards and wore their hair loose and full.

"You gonna be 'English'?" cried Shoo-Fly.

Jonas only laughed.

The next day Shoo-Fly saw the new children again — at school. Just before the last bell rang, their mother drove up in a big green car and they jumped out. Their mother talked to Miss Weber, then drove away.

Shoo-Fly and Reuben and the twins went to Meadowbrook School. It had one room and six grades. Most of the children were Amish, but not all. Beck and Bib went to a small junior high for Amish children. Shoo-Fly liked her teacher even if she wasn't Amish. Miss Weber's hair hung in soft waves to her shoulders. Her cheeks were pink and she wore pretty silk dresses.

At school, Shoo-Fly was still Suzanna. Miss Weber did not like nicknames.

When school took up, all the children came running in pell-mell, and took their seats. There in the empty seat beside Suzanna sat the new girl. Betty Ferguson, Miss Weber said her name was. She was in the fourth grade too. Suzanna paid no attention to her.

Until recess, when Betty smiled and put her arm around Suzanna.

"I didn't know you could speak English," said Betty.

"Why, sure," said Suzanna. "Why not?"

"You'll be my girlfriend, won't you?" asked Betty.

The others were calling. Suzanna ran to the cupboard and got ball and bat and baseball gloves. She ran out and started a ball game in the high grass. All the Amish girls were good ball players. The new children stood and watched.

Suzanna loved to play ball. She bossed the other children around, even the "English" boys. In the middle of the game, a gray car drove up and stopped. The children looked, then went on with their game. A man got out with a large black box and started fussing.

"It's a camera!" Amos Zook said, just loud enough for all to hear. Amos was the son of the Amish Bishop in this district, so the children listened. The game broke up. The children huddled together, heads turned, a whisper or two, then they scattered like dry leaves in a gusty wind. One minute they were there, and the next minute when the man had his camera all set and looked up, they were gone. There was nothing to take a picture of.

Suzanna ran the fastest. She took the twins by the hand and dragged them inside the school. Miss Weber came to see.

Shoo-Fly said, "Photographs are wicked. We all ran. He was a tourist!"

Miss Weber smiled. She understood.

"But what did they run for?"

There was that new girl again, wanting to know everything.

"Photographs are wicked," said Shoo-Fly. "It says so in the Bible!"

"Oh!" said Betty. "Does it?"

After the man left, the boys began playing *horse*. With

binders' twine for harness, they drove each other madly about, stamping and prancing. Then the bell rang and it was time to go in. The children lined up at the iron pump to wash. Amos Zook, John Esh and Reuben pumped. The children washed their hands and drank from cupped fingers. They ran indoors, panting.

That day was a happy one for Suzanna, because Miss Weber gave her a new storybook to take home. She looked at the title, *Rebecca of Sunnybrook Farm!* Rebecca! It must be about an Amish girl! There were many Amish Rebeccas. She patted the book lovingly.

The new girl looked at it too.

"That book's no good," she said. "It's stupid! Why don't you get a *mystery* book? Or a *horse* book? I like *horse* books, I just love horses!"

It was time to go. Three little Amish girls took brooms, dustpans and dustcloths to clean the schoolroom. Suzanna stepped on a chair at the back of the room. She got the twins' bonnets down from the shelf, and her own. She looked at the initials inside to get the right ones. She got Reuben's hat down too.

The boys ran for their homemade scooters. Quickly Reuben took off shoes and stockings and hung them across the scooter handle. He set his lunchbox at the base, and with the other boys, went dashing off, coattails flying and black felt hats tipped on backs of their heads. The girls were soon left far behind.

"Go ahead!" Suzanna told her little sisters. "Go ahead with the other girls. I'm not in a hurry today."

They started down the road, a colorful group of bonneted

and aproned little girls wearing dark bonnets, sweaters and shawls. A few had black shoes and stockings, but most were barefoot. Suzanna brought up the rear.

"I hope that new girl won't come and talk to me," she said to herself. Looking back, she saw Betty Ferguson still in the schoolroom, talking to Miss Weber. "Teacher's pet!" she said aloud.

Shoo-Fly walked slowly, reading her book. It was not about an Amish girl, after all. But oh, it was good, good, good! How would she ever find time to read it? Once home, there were all those chores waiting, nothing but work, work, work, no time to read at all. Mam and Dat thought books were a waste of time. So her nose dipped lower and lower and her steps grew slower and slower. Better read while she had the chance.

Suddenly she bumped into something. She looked up and found herself in the ditch, with her nose against a tree! Oh dear, did anybody see her? They would say she was *ferhoodlt!* Back in the road, a sharp honk made her jump to one side. It was that new girl's mother, heading for the school.

She saw the Amish girls ahead huddled in a group. She closed her book and ran ahead to join them. They had stopped at a telephone pole. This was something new to them, as none of the Amish farms had telephones. A new line had just been put in to the Fergusons' house. Shoo-Fly knew all about it. A telephone was something you talked into. You talked to people far away. The talk went over the telephone wires. If you put your ear up close to the pole, you could hear what the people were saying. The Amish girls listened one by one, but they all shook their heads.

"We can't make out what they're sayin'."

"Here! Let me once!" Shoo-Fly did everything with vigor. She pushed the other girls away, shoved her bonnet back and put her ear close to the pole.

"They're talking in Greek," she announced, her eyes open wide. "No, it's French, I think. Wait a minute, it sounds like Italian! They say there's a bad snowstorm over there and everybody is snowed under and an avalanche is sliding down the mountain and going to bury a whole town full of people . . ."

Her eyes gleamed as the story got bigger and bigger.

"I don't believe a word of it!" snapped Katie Zook. "You're makin' all that up."

"Yes, well," Shoo-Fly went on, "it could be any language at all. . . . Miss Weber said we've got Greeks and French and Italians and Polish and all kinds of people in our country, the whole world is not all just Pennsylvania Dutch like you, Katie Zook. . . ."

But Katie was far on down the road, not listening at all.

Just then a car came speeding up. It was the big green one again. Mrs. Ferguson had picked up Betty and her little brother and sister at school and was taking them home. The car stopped beside the group of girls.

"Suzanna, would you like a ride home?" asked Mrs. Ferguson. She opened the car door and Betty begged her to get in.

The temptation was too great to be resisted. Katie Zook was not asked to ride, only Suzanna Fisher. *I'll show her!* thought Shoo-Fly. The next minute she was in the car, sitting on the shiny soft green cushion beside Betty. Before Mrs. Ferguson started on, Shoo-Fly heard the twins crying and the taunts of the other girls.

"Suzanna wants to be 'English'!"

"I'll tell your Mam! You'll get a licking!"

But she held up her head in pride. She was the *only* one asked to ride.

It was Shoo-Fly's first ride in an automobile. The car slid along so nice and smooth and even. There were no bumps at all. Everything went by so fast — the trees, the fences, the corn in the fields, a house or two — she could hardly see them. Betty kept on talking, but she did not hear. Then all at once she was frightened. The car went fast and kept on going faster. Mrs. Ferguson wasn't looking at the road. She kept turning around and talking to the girls in the back seat.

And there ahead, out from a side lane came an Amish buggy. The car almost hit it! Shoo-Fly trembled in fright. Why, it was her own lane and that was Grossmama in her buggy driving her horse Sonny Boy. Shoo-Fly gasped! Her face went white. The car came near to hitting Grossmama!

The danger was over now. The car had passed the buggy safely. Shoo-Fly had waved weakly, but Grossmama did not see her. Grossmama did not look at people riding in cars.

Then Mrs. Ferguson slowed down. "I went past your lane," she said. "I'll have to turn around. We'll go in. I want to meet your mother."

Shoo-Fly could not answer. She could not seem to find words.

Mam was in the house yard taking down the clothes. She had washed that morning. She had to wash three times a week. Somebody had let the geese out. There were thirty of them. They were supposed to stay in their own fenced field. Now they were all over the yard, cackling and making a mess on the cement sidewalk. Mam was waiting for the children to come home to pen them up again.

The place looked terrible.

Mrs. Ferguson stopped in the barnyard beside the row of martin box poles. Mam came out to meet the car. She had her white prayer covering on, tied in a bow hanging below her chin. But her dress and apron were not clean. She probably thought it was an egg customer. What she saw surprised her.

"You must be Mrs. Fisher," said Mrs. Ferguson, brightly. "I'm your new neighbor, Dolly Ferguson."

Politely, Mam shook her hand. "Pleased to meet you, Mrs. Ferguson."

The air was filled with ice.

"I brought your little girl home from school," said Mrs. Ferguson, "in my car."

"I see you did." Mam's mouth was a thin line. Her face froze. Shoo-Fly climbed out. Mam looked down at her daughter. "Suzanna rode home in your *car?*"

"Yes, she hitchhiked with me!" said Mrs. Ferguson with a laugh. "Is that something terrible?"

Mam looked at Suzanna again.

"I thought she knew better," she said slowly. Then to Mrs. Ferguson, "She's young yet, but she'll learn."

"Learn what?" asked Mrs. Ferguson, baffled.

"Not to ride in cars," said Mam, quietly and with pride. "It is not our way. We do not ride in cars. We are Amish."

"Oh! I'm sorry," said Mrs. Ferguson. "Is it wicked?"

"It is not necessary," said Mam. "We ride in cars only in case of emergency. Please do not pick her up again. Suzanna has two good legs. She can walk."

Coldly Mrs. Ferguson turned away. How could she ever be friends with these queer people? When you try to do them a kindness. . . .

Shoo-Fly walked in the house slowly, hugging her new book in her arms. Reuben and the twins came home, then the older girls. They all made a dash for the big pretzel can in the kitchen. They filled their mouths with salty pretzels and all talked at once — in English.

Mam came in frowning. She heard their English talk.

"We are Dutch," she said. "We don't speak English here."

The talk simmered down into the soft tones of Pennsylvania Dutch.

Shoo-Fly grabbed a handful of pretzels and stuffed them into the secret pocket under her apron. She took another handful and stuffed them into her mouth. Mam looked so cross, Shoo-Fly was afraid to say a word. She slipped out the side door when no one was looking.

She would go and see Grossmama. Grossmama was a good friend in time of need.

Grossmama and Aunt Suzanna lived in the Grossdawdy house. The Fishers' house was a double one, two houses joined together. Grossdawdy, who was dead now, had built his house first. Then when he got too old to farm, he joined another house on, for his youngest son, Rufus. That was Shoo-Fly's father, whom the children called Dat. Aunt Suzanna was Dat's sister, and little Suzanna, or Shoo-Fly, had been named for her. Aunt Suzanna and Grossmama lived together now in the Grossdawdy house.

Shoo-Fly ran around the corner and in at the door, but the big kitchen was empty. Where was Grossmama?

There was her rocking chair beside the window, with the ferns and potted plants. There was her sewing basket, her thimble and scissors. The fire was burning in the range and something was cooking in the big pot. The kettle was singing comfortably. The room was quiet, peaceful, still. Only the big clock on the high shelf made a noise, ticking steadily. Then it growled and struck the hour, a lonely sound.

Shoo-Fly's heart sank and tears came to her eyes. Where was Grossmama? She wanted to be a little girl again, to sit on Grossmama's lap and feel her warm arms around her. She wanted to talk things over.

But the house was empty. She called up the stairway. No one answered. Grossmama was gone.

Then Shoo-Fly remembered. She had seen Sonny Boy and the buggy go out the lane as she drove in with Mrs. Ferguson. Grossmama went riding in her buggy whenever she wanted to. She never told where she was going. Maybe she went to see Great-Grossmama or Uncle John, or the doctor or to the store. Maybe she just went to pick up Aunt Suzanna at the gift shop where she worked.

Grossmama would soon be back. She *had* to get back before sundown. She had no lamps on her buggy. She always stayed home after dark. So Shoo-Fly waited. She sat on the couch and waited in the gathering darkness. She ate her pretzels one by one. Then at last Grossmama came.

In she came, little, sprightly, brisk Grossmama, as chipper as a grasshopper. She took off her bonnet and shawl and hung them up. Then in came the twins, Punkin and Puddin, prancing and capering. The twins squealing and giggling. The twins chattering their heads off! Aunt Suzanna came in too.

125

Nobody noticed Shoo-Fly curled up on the couch. Or if they saw her, they ignored her. Grossmama started supper, while Aunt Suzanna pumped up the gas lamp and lighted it. Then she hung it over the table.

The twins were going to stay for supper. The twins had brought their nightgowns with them . . . they were going to stay all night . . . at Grossmama's. . . . The twins were spoiled rotten, Mam always said.

Grossmama put wood on the fire, stirred the pot with a big spoon, then sat down in her rocker and took the twins on her lap. Big seven-year-old girls, two of them on her lap at once! She rocked them back and forth. She began to sing to them:

Aw, ba, za,
De kots lawft im shna,
D'r shna gat avech,
De kots lawft in dreck . . .
A, B, C,
The cat walks in the snow,
The snow goes away
And the cat walks in the mud,
Jumps over the stump
with a bag full of rags,
Jumps over the barn
with a bag full of fire!

It was too much. Shoo-Fly couldn't stand it. She got up and started for the door.

"Where are you going, Susie?" called Grossmama, looking up.

But it was too late now.

Shoo-Fly did not answer.

She went out and banged the door behind her.

Shoo-Fly did not get the threatened licking, nor did she ride in the Fergusons' car again. The next day at school, her life was miserable. The children teased her and never let up.

"Suzanna's trying to be English!" they cried.

She met every taunt with, "*Ach,* be still!" but that did not help much. Her only comfort was in her library book. That day she almost *ran* home from school. She couldn't wait to read more about Rebecca.

At home, the first thing she saw was that the yard was spotless. The geese were all in the goose run, and the walks had been scrubbed clean. There were three Amish buggies in the barnyard. That meant company.

Before she went in, she took her crow out of his pen and turned him loose. He flew to a treetop and when she called him, he flew down and landed on her shoulder. He sat on her finger and ate corn out of her hand. But he would not let the twins hold him at all. He pecked at them instead. Before she put him back in his pen, she decided to name him Jackie.

She went in the kettle house, opened the kitchen door and took a peek. It was a quilting. Mam had her newest quilt on the frame in the front room. All seven aunts must be in there quilting. They were all talking at once. It sounded like birds making noises in a tree. The kitchen was big, as big as two average kitchens. It never looked bigger than now. It was filled with children. All the aunts had children, mostly babies . . . cousins . . . To Shoo-Fly babies meant bottles to be filled and diapers to be changed. She knew all about that! They were all crying and whining and fussing. She stepped over their heads, slid past the door opening into the front room and headed for the stairs.

There was only one thing to do — disappear. Hide where nobody would find her. How wonderful to have the library book! It was a good chance to read. The aunts must have been there for dinner. She glanced at the sink in passing. Why stay around when all those stacks and mounds of dishes were waiting? They hadn't even washed their own dishes or swept the floor after eating! Could it be they expected certain girls to come home from school and do it? Let them do it themselves! And if they stayed for supper, let them carry in their own wood, cook their food and wash dishes again!

Shoo-Fly crept quietly up the stairs.

She found her book and began to read. She changed to her old clothes as slowly as she could, reading as fast as she could. She was living with a non-Amish Rebecca on a non-Amish farm . . . oh, it was wonderful! This book-Rebecca rode on a stage, not in a buggy. . . .

Suddenly a voice broke into her dream.

"*Suz-an-na! Suz-an-na!*" It was Mam's voice calling. "*Suzanna! Run down cellar and bring me a big jar of chow-chow!*"

Shoo-Fly had to think quickly. They'd find her up here in the bedroom, that's for sure. Beck and Bib would soon be home and come up here to change clothes. *They* could help Mam. It was time to disappear. But how? Where? Shoo-Fly had a number of favorite hiding places, but how to get to them?

Then an idea hit her. Clutching her book under her arm,

she crept into the boys' bedroom. It was dark and spooky. Mam always kept the shades pulled. She stumbled and fell over big boys' shoes left in the middle of the floor, then got up. She saw a flashlight on Jonas' washstand and decided to borrow it. The window over the one-story kettle house could be opened. She could jump down on the lower roof and then from there to the ground. No sooner said than done.

Lucky she was a good jumper. She had had plenty of practice in the barn, taking dares from Jonas and Reuben. But in the barn there was hay to land on. Not hard ground barely covered with grass. The geese had nibbled it bare. She came down with a thump and frightened the geese. They all began to gobble. *Be quiet, you noisy things!* Her book fell, then the flashlight. *Ach! did I break it?* She picked them up and ran. She must get out of the goose run before anybody saw her. Pretzel chased her and began to bark.

Where to go? Which hidey-hole would be best?

Being the middle child in a family of nine, Shoo-Fly had problems. Her two big sisters and two big brothers thought she was too little to do what they did. Her two little sisters and two little brothers thought she was too big. She often found it hard to survive in a world all her own — smack in the middle.

The hidey-holes were a big help.

Which should it be? Where should she go? She had to think fast, before she got caught. Over to Grossmama's? No, not after last night. Behind the egg crates in the chicken house? No, it was too lousy there. Up in the haymow? The barn was full of tobacco now and smelled awful. Up in the cherry tree? They might see her there. How about the family buggy? Not Grossmama's but Mam's. It was in the barn. Mam would not be going anywhere as long as the aunts were there. No sooner said than done.

Shoo-Fly slipped in the side door of the barn and climbed into the buggy. Lucky she brought the flashlight along. It wasn't broken at all. Then she heard a noise, a squeaky noise, a whiny noise. Was it a cat mewing? She flashed her light on the buggy floor.

"Jeepers! Look there!" she cried. "It's Becky Green-Eyes and she's got kittens!"

There in a nice soft nest on the old horse blanket was Beck's cat that Jonas had named, with five baby kittens! They were squirming and mewing. Their eyes weren't open yet. She'd tell Beck so she could feed them — but not now. Later on. They wouldn't bother her. She shoved them over out of the way.

She curled up on the floor and pillowed her head on the seat cushion. It was dark and spooky, but homelike and cozy. She flashed the light on. She could read comfortably. No one would find her. She entered another world.

The book-Rebecca liked to read books too, dozens of books that Shoo-Fly had never even heard of. She had problems too, she was one of a big family. . . . She had aunts, only two, though, one pleasant and one unpleasant. . . .

It was the crow cawing loudly that brought Shoo-Fly back to life.

Jonas had been sent to find her. He thought of a quick way to locate her. He let the crow out of its pen and began to chase and tease it. The crow protested noisily, and his angry caws brought Shoo-Fly running. Pretzel was jumping and barking madly.

"Where have you *been?*" cried Punkin.

"We hunted everywhere for you," said Puddin.

Shoo-Fly put the crow back in his pen. The buggies and the aunts and the babies were all gone now. She hadn't even heard them go. Somebody had cooked supper. The family was waiting. They couldn't pray without her. She rushed to her seat on the bench, bowed her head and closed her eyes.

Her heart was beating fast under her black apron.

"Oh, God!" she prayed. "Don't let them ask me any questions!"

◆ ◆ ◆

Shoo-Fly was alone in the big kitchen. She heard a timid knock and went to the door. There was Betty Ferguson. Nobody had invited her.

"I came for a visit," said Betty.

Betty was dressed in T-shirt and blue jeans. Her head was a bird's nest of curls. Shoo-Fly opened the door and Betty came in. They stood and looked at each other. What would Mam say?

Shoo-Fly went back to her work. She was making shoo-fly pies, four of them today. Beck had lighted the gas oven and helped her mix the pastry. Now they were ready to put in.

"What are you doing?" asked Betty.

"Baking pies," said Shoo-Fly. "To sell at the pie stand on the highway."

A row of pies already baked stood on the counter.

"What's this?" Betty pointed to bread pans sitting on the back of the range. They were filled with dough set to rise. The dough was white and soft and puffy. It was rising up over the tops.

"That's bread," said Shoo-Fly. "Mam's baking bread to sell, too."

"Do you sell pies and bread?" asked Betty.

"Yes, good homemade bread," said Shoo-Fly. "I got to go to the pie stand tomorrow." As she told Betty about it, it made her feel very important.

"It looks good," said Betty. "So soft and puffy . . ." She reached out and pushed her forefinger down in the middle of each puffy loaf before Shoo-Fly could stop her. The puffs began to sink slowly and the dough went soggy.

"*Ach!*" cried Shoo-Fly. "Look now what you've done. You've ruined Mam's bread. You're not to touch it. When it goes once down, it won't come up again. It stays flat and has to be fed to the hogs."

Betty said, "Oh, does it?" She tossed her head. "How should I know?"

Bib came in first, then Beck. They both looked at the sunken loaves and scolded. Then Mam came down from upstairs. She looked at the bread and then at Shoo-Fly.

"What happened?" she asked.

Shoo-Fly pointed to Betty. "She did it. She didn't know . . . ."

Mam frowned and said nothing. She put the shoo-fly pies in the oven and told the two girls to go outside and play.

Betty began to cry. Shoo-Fly put an arm around her. She felt sorry for her. Poor Betty didn't know any better. They went outside and saw the twins playing. They were baking cake, they said.

"I found six eggs in the hen house," said Punkin.

"We mixed them with mud . . . it makes very good cake," said Puddin.

"We put corn on the top just for fancy," said Punkin.

"So it's mud-corn cake," said Puddin.

Shoo-Fly and Betty had to laugh.

There was the crow sitting on the fence.

"Let's play with Jackie," said Shoo-Fly.

She called and the bird came and perched on her finger. She fed it some corn. The crow made talking noises.

"Say *hel-lo!*" said Shoo-Fly.

The crow cocked his head and looked at Shoo-Fly. *Hel-lo,* he cawed.

"Hello, Jackie!" said Shoo-Fly.

"Hel-lo Jack-ie!" answered the crow.

Betty laughed nervously. "I never knew a crow could talk," she said. She wasn't sure she liked the crow at all.

"Every morning he sits by my window and calls me," said Shoo-Fly. "He tells me when it's time to get up. He won't stop until I come out and feed him."

The crow went flying up in the air. It came down and landed on the clothesline. It began to peck at the clothespins. Shoo-Fly chased it.

"Go away, Jackie! Let Mam's clothespins alone."

"What's he doing?" asked Betty.

"He likes to peck the clothespins off," said Shoo-Fly, "and hide them. He even takes our hankies and hides them!"

The crow flapped down again. He landed on Betty's head, in the middle of her curls. She screamed and fought it off. She was terrified.

"Ach!" cried Shoo-Fly, laughing. "You look so *strubbly . . . ."*

She chased the bird away. He flew up into the treetops. Then Rags and Hayfork came running.

133

"Want a ride? Want a ride?" they called. "Old Bug is waiting!"

"Take off your shoes and socks," said Shoo-Fly. "It's lots more fun."

Betty did as she was told. The Amish children hated shoes and seldom wore them at home, often going barefoot even in cold weather.

Shoo-Fly and Betty ran up the bank slope to the open barn door. The barn was built on the slope of a bank. That is why it was called a bank barn. There stood an old broken-down buggy without a top. It had no shafts, no seat, only a board to sit on, but its wheels were still in running order. Rags had tied a rope to the front axle to guide it. The children climbed on and were ready to go. The twins and the dog Pretzel came too. It made a big load.

Rags gave a push and down the hill they went, laughing and screaming. Down the steep hill and into the grassy field, where Old Bug stopped. Pretzel barked loudly. They all piled out and pulled Old Bug up the hill again. Down they went over and over. It was fun.

"Oh, come on," said Shoo-Fly, getting tired. "Let's go over to Grossmama's."

Grossmama and Aunt Suzanna had been cleaning house. One of the upstairs windows was open. Jackie, the crow, had spotted the girls and now started swooping down over their heads.

"Oh, I'm scared! Make him stop!" Betty covered her head with her arms. "He'll get in my hair again. He'll scratch my eyes out!"

"He *likes* you!" said Shoo-Fly. "He won't hurt you. Don't be afraid."

"But I don't like *him!*" wailed Betty. "Make him go away."

Shoo-Fly took a broom from Grossmama's porch and waved it at the crow. He lighted on the end of the broom and made the girls laugh. Then she banged the broom on the porch post and he flew off cawing noisily.

"He's mad!" said Shoo-Fly. "He's scolding us!"

Up and around in the air flew the crow, cawing and squawking.

"Yes, well, let us alone once," said Shoo-Fly.

The crow circled around high overhead, and then, with a swoop, sailed in at the open upstairs window of Grossmama's house.

Shoo-Fly gasped. How terrible now! It was the window of the "good room," the room where all the treasures were kept.

"I must run and tell Grossmama! I must tell Aunt Suzanna, I must shoo him out of there!" Shoo-Fly ran into the house with frightened Betty at her heels.

No one was there. Where had people gone? Were they out in the garden somewhere? Shoo-Fly opened the stair door and ran up the steps. The door to the "good room" was always kept closed and the shades pulled down. But now they were up and the window open to air the room out.

There was the crow in the middle of the floor.

"Caw, caw!" he said, cocking his eye at Shoo-Fly.

"*Ach,* what a wicked bird you are!" cried Shoo-Fly. "See what you've done! Shoo out of here! Shoo on out and stay out where you belong." She shooed and chased, the crow flapped and flopped and knocked things over. At last he found the open window and flew out, but not till after he had done a great deal of damage.

The "good room" was the place where treasures were kept. There were two handsome bureaus and two cedar chests belonging to Dat's two unmarried sisters, Aunt Suzanna and Aunt Leah. Aunt Leah was away working on a farm. The chests and bureaus were full of handmade quilts and sheets, pillowcases and towels. On the tops stood beautiful dishes and glassware, vases, cups and saucers, pitchers, water sets, serving dishes. All these things were gifts the aunts had kept since they were little girls. It was their pay for staying with their parents and taking care of them. It was their dowry for their marriage.

Aunt Suzanna's choicest treasure was a bunch of artificial fruit — grapes, peaches, lemons and bananas — that had been given her when she was ten. They were beautiful because they looked so real.

Shoo-Fly stared at them now in dismay. The crow had ruined them. He had pecked holes in the peaches, scattered the grapes and broken open the bananas. Worst of all, in his mad flight about the room, he had left a trail of broken glass and china behind him.

Shoo-Fly felt like crying.

"*Ai-y-y!* What will Grossmama say? What will Aunt Suzanna say? Now they will want to get rid of him. That's for sure!"

Betty put her arm around her.

"But it wasn't *your* fault the crow got in," she said. "Somebody left the window open . . ."

But Shoo-Fly's heart sank.

"It's my crow," she said sadly. "Nobody likes him but me."

It was an anticlimax.

Shoo-Fly had wanted to tell Betty about the "good room"

and how sacred it was. The room was so elegant, it always sent shivers up and down Shoo-Fly's spine. All the furniture used to belong to dead people. None of the treasures was ever touched. They were keepsakes to be kept. Every little hanky, every dish, every vase had the name of its donor marked on it in remembrance. In the "good room," beauty and sentiment, denied in Amish living, were enshrined and held captive.

Shoo-Fly wanted to tell Betty Ferguson this. It was something important in her life. Something that Betty Ferguson had never seen or heard of. Something that "English" people did not know about.

But now it was spoiled. The "good room" had been invaded and desecrated. And by that mean old crow, Jackie! Was he really as bad and mean as everybody said?

Shoo-Fly shrugged her shoulders.

I like him anyhow, she thought. *I won't let him go. He's mine. He's the only thing I've got that nobody else wants.*

Aloud she said, "Let's go quick before Grossmama gets back."

They ran back home and there in the house yard, another calamity met their eyes. Most of Mam's nice clean washing was lying on the ground. More of Jackie's mischief. The crow had taken out all the clothespins and hid them somewhere. Jonas was right to call him a thief. Mam would be furious!

The twins came screaming, "Who took our play dishes? Who took our play dishes?"

But Shoo-Fly did not linger. Out in the barnyard, she suddenly had an idea. "Let's go horseback riding," she said.

"Oh, I'd be afraid to," said Betty.

"But you said you *liked* horses," said Shoo-Fly.

"Only in books," said Betty. "I just *love* horse books."

"We've got five horses and two mules," said Shoo-Fly. "I can hitch up a horse, feed it, harness it and ride horseback."

Betty looked at her in astonishment.

"Come, I'll show you a real horse." Shoo-Fly went in the stable and brought out old Lady. Lady was nearly twenty years old, no longer able to work. But the children loved her.

"Come, let's go for a ride!" cried Shoo-Fly.

She led Lady to the fence and climbed up on her back. Punkin and Puddin came too and climbed on behind. Betty climbed on the fence and they all pulled her up. She was up there, but sitting backwards, and they could not turn her around.

The horse was so high, it was scary to Betty. The horse was so wide, it was like being on a roof. Then the whole thing began to move and bounce up and down. Betty hung on tight. She tried not to scream, but wailing words burst from her mouth. "I want off! Take me off!" cried Betty.

Slowly at first, then round and round the barnyard the old horse went. It was a good thing Betty was wedged in tightly, she could not possibly fall. Then — well, it wasn't so bad after all. Just when she was beginning to enjoy it, a green car drove into the barnyard.

It was Mrs. Ferguson come to take Betty home.

"Why does *she* have to come?" asked Shoo-Fly. "Can't you ever walk?" After all, Betty lived only ten minutes away.

"Let me down! Let me down!" screamed Betty. "That's Mommy!"

They all slid off and ran to the car.

Mrs. Ferguson stared in dismay. She hardly knew her own

daughter. Betty's clothes were soiled and dirty. Her hair was wild and her face was black. Her feet were bare and dirty too.

"*Where* are your shoes and socks, Betty?" her mother demanded.

Shoo-Fly decided to speak up for her.

"She took them off," she said. "We hate shoes."

"I see you do," said Mrs. Ferguson, looking at all the bare, dirty feet.

"We can run faster without shoes," said Shoo-Fly.

"Betty, where are your shoes and socks?" asked Mrs. Ferguson.

It took a long time to find them. Then Betty got in the car with her mother.

"Good-by, Betty!" cried Shoo-Fly and the twins. "Come again soon."

"I never had so much fun in my whole life!" Betty called back, as the car went out the lane.

That evening Grossmama came over and reported the damage in the "good room." She said Aunt Suzanna wept over the ruined artificial fruit. Shoo-Fly told her she had found the crow inside and had shooed it out.

Everybody said the crow was bad, and Mam said she was tired of finding her washing on the ground every week and the small pieces gone. Dat said it was time to get rid of the crow. Jonas said, "Don't worry! He'll fly away one of these days and we'll never see him again." They all said such bad things about the crow that Shoo-Fly's heart sank.

What would happen to her pet?

The next day Mam took Shoo-Fly to the pie stand after

school, and said she would come for her later. It was her first time at the pie stand alone. She felt very sad after Mam drove home and left her. She tried to remember her instructions. Then she sat down and watched the cars whizz by.

Nobody stopped. Shoo-Fly was weaving pot-holders. Beck had showed her how. She hated to weave and the pot-holders always ended up crooked. But Mam said she could sell them and keep half the money. So she set to work. There was nobody to talk to.

After a long time a car stopped. The people asked questions. They asked her name and how old she was. They bought home-made bread. Another car stopped. A woman bought bread and two pot-holders. Shoo-Fly took the money and put it in her purse. It hung from its long strap over her shoulder. She opened and shut it carefully.

The cars went zipping by. When they did not stop, Shoo-Fly wished they would. When they did, she wished they wouldn't. It frightened her. It was hard to talk to strangers.

Everybody wanted bread and it was soon sold out. Everybody wanted pot-holders and she couldn't make them fast enough. Nobody wanted pie today. The flies came and buzzed around. Would Mam never come? And what would she say when she saw the pies were not sold?

Now it was lonelier than ever. It was getting dark too. The cars had turned their lights on. The headlights shone in her eyes and blinded her. When was Mam coming? Why did Mam keep her waiting so long? She wanted to go home. She wanted to stay at home and never go away again.

Then all at once, two big headlights like the eyes of a monster came right toward her. Another car was going the other way, so the monster turned aside to avoid hitting it. A screech of the brakes . . . a loud crash . . . it came to a quick stop — just in time.

Shoo-Fly saw it coming, jumped back, terrified, and started to run. Anywhere, anywhere, to get away from the monster . . . . Crying and sobbing she stumbled across the field. . . .

Then a man's voice spoke and a man's hand caught her by the arm.

"Don't run away," the man said. "It's all over. I didn't mean to frighten you. There's no harm done — my brakes are good. Come on back now, Shoo-Fly Girl, I won't hurt you."

She knew him at once. It was the Mystery Man from Massachusetts, who liked shoo-fly pie so much. He was the one who had given her that terrible nickname. Now he had almost run over her. If she had not run. . . .

Then she looked. The pie stand stood where it always stood. It was not hurt at all. Nothing was disturbed. The big black monster's headlights threw a bright light on everything — on all the pies and cakes that nobody wanted.

"Well, Shoo-Fly Girl, that was a close shave!" said the man calmly. "That crazy driver was heading straight for me and I had to get out of his way. I'm sorry I frightened you."

He pointed to the pies. "How's business today — good? 'Bout time for you to go home, isn't it? Nobody here with you today? How are the pies, good?"

Shoo-Fly could not answer any of his questions. She was still white and shaken. Why didn't Mam come and take her and the pies and cakes home?

"I'll take everything," the man said, but Shoo-Fly did not hear.

He put some bills in her hand and started to put the pies in a box in his car.

Then Shoo-Fly heard the sound of a horse's hoofs and the next minute Mam got out of her buggy. Shoo-Fly ran to her mother's arms and burst into tears. "He tried to run me over!" she cried.

The man talked to Mam, explaining everything. He ended up saying, "I bought her out."

"*Ach,* but . . ." Mrs. Fisher began. "You must have a big family, to eat all those pies and cakes. . . ."

The man turned toward her. His face had a stricken look.

"Yes — big family . . ." he said.

He started up his car and drove away.

"Don't make me go again! Don't make me go again!" begged Shoo-Fly all the way home.

The world was full of peril and risk, temptation and evil. All her life, Shoo-Fly had been warned of the dangers of worldliness. From the safe and quiet world of her home, she had taken her first step outside, and she did not like what she saw there. She crept home, hurt and bewildered.

Then another blow came, worse than the first. It came close, not striking her directly, but her brother Jonas, and that was almost the same as herself. For he was the favorite of all her brothers and sisters, the only one who understood her.

Dat and Jonas and Rags had gone over to Uncle Chris's to help fill the silo with green corn. The farm seemed empty and lifeless without them. In the late afternoon Shoo-Fly went out to gather the eggs. Some of the hens liked to lay in the barn, so she went in to look for eggs. Shoo-Fly could not climb up on the rafters now and jump down in the soft hay any more. All the upper part was filled with drying tobacco.

She walked around slowly. Becky Green-Eyes and her kittens came up mewing, so she got some milk and fed them. Now and then she found an egg and put it in her basket. The whole place was quiet. Off in the field she could hear the crows cawing and knew that Jackie must be with them.

Suddenly a strange sound met her ears. She stood still and listened. Was she dreaming? Was it music? Where was it coming from? It was very soft, and sometimes it nearly died away. Then it came on louder and sweeter again. Was it . . . could it be . . . a radio? Miss Weber had one at school, the only one Shoo-Fly had ever heard. Amish families did not have them. The Bishop told them they were not necessary.

The music was light and lively. It made Shoo-Fly feel happy, almost like dancing on her toes. *Where* was it coming from? It must be *secret* music, hidden away somewhere. Forgetting about the eggs, Shoo-Fly searched. She knew all the dark corners and out-of-the-way hiding places. She crept about quietly, in the harness room and out, in the stable and out, in the egg room, the granary, and then in the old carriage shed. It was like a game, playing now "hot," now "cold." She felt herself getting warmer and warmer, as she came up to the old broken buggy. It was Old Bug, the one the children played with. A big canvas had been thrown over the half-broken frame, to make a shelter. She crept around to the back and looked in.

There sat Jonas, big fifteen-year-old Jonas, huddled in a heap. On the seat of the buggy was a radio, set on the floor.

"*Ach!*" cried Shoo-Fly. "So it's you! I found you once."

"Sh! Sh!" said Jonas, finger to his lips. "Why do *you* have to come here and spoil everything?"

"I . . . I heard the music and . . ." began Shoo-Fly.

"Well now, clear out! Get going! Go on away and don't come around here again!"

"But I thought you went to Uncle Chris's to help fill the silo," said Shoo-Fly.

"I did and I worked and I came away," said Jonas. "They've got all the help they need without me."

Shoo-Fly pointed to the forbidden radio.

"*Where did you get it?*" she asked in a whisper.

"I *borrowed* it," said Jonas. "And don't you go tell on me!"

Shoo-Fly shook her head. She and Jonas were friends. They liked each other. She could count on Jonas more than on any of her other brothers or sisters. She could not be disloyal. Jonas was a big tease, but most of the time he was good to her. She climbed up in the buggy and sat down.

"What will Dat say if he finds out?" she asked.

"He won't say much, he'll just smash it."

"What will the Bishop say?" she whispered.

"I won't tell him," said Jonas.

"But if he finds out?" said Shoo-Fly.

"He won't, unless some little squirt squeals on me," said Jonas.

"On that one at school last year I heard all about space and rockets and missiles. . . ." He turned the knob and the tune changed to a loud noisy one. He tuned it lower. "That's *jazz!*" he said with a grin.

"*Ach!* I don't like it!" said Shoo-Fly, frightened. "Turn it off! It hurts my ears terrible!"

144

"It's all the rage . . ." said Jonas, "Bill Ferguson tells me."

Shoo-Fly knew that Betty had an older brother named Bill. "Did you borrow it from Bill?" she asked.

Jonas closed his lips tight. "I'm not telling," he said. Then he looked at his sister and blurted out, "Sometimes I wish I wasn't Amish at all. I *like* TV and radios and cars!"

"*Ach*, Jonas!" gasped Shoo-Fly. "*Don't* say that!"

"It's true," said Jonas. "I can't help it."

"Where have you seen TV?" asked Shoo-Fly.

"At a tavern in town," said Jonas. "Bill took me. Bill wants me to go away with him . . . to Canada, maybe. . . . He has some rich relatives living there . . . we could do as we please. . . . There are no bishops up there."

"*Ach*, Jonas!" cried Shoo-Fly in distress. "*Don't* say that!"

Jonas had not meant to tell her at all. But she was his trusting friend, and he had to tell somebody. He felt better after he had blurted it out. Then, even in the dim light of the shed, he saw the shocked look on his sister's face and it frightened him.

"Oh, *shucks!*" he said. "Forget it! I'm not going, don't get so scared. It's just that sometimes I *wish* I could!"

He had turned the radio off now.

"Don't tell anybody where I keep it," said Jonas.

"I won't," said Shoo-Fly. Then she had an idea. "If . . . if you like music . . ." she began, "why don't you get a mouth organ instead? The Bishop says harmonicas are O.K."

"Huh!" snorted Jonas. "Kid stuff! Who wants one of them?"

"But you can play pretty tunes on it . . ." said Shoo-Fly.

Somehow she wanted to help her brother, but how?

"Take your eggs and go in the house," said Jonas. "I'm

going back to Uncle Chris's. This is *our* secret now. Will you promise me you won't tell?"

Shoo-Fly nodded, her face serious.

There was no one around as she slowly made her way to the back door. But her heart was heavy with the burden that Jonas had placed there.

❧ Author Biographies ❧

Elizabeth Coatsworth (1893-1986) was an author whose primary interest was the ever-changing America she grew up in. She wrote about a diverse range of subjects, from the Vikings when they invaded Ireland in *The Wanderers* to the legendary inhabitants of the Norway's fjords and mountains in *Troll Weather*. She always returned, however, to the vast American landscape for inspiration. Although her 1931 Newbery-winning story *The Cat Who Went to Heaven* is set in medieval Japan, the United States, especially the New England coastline, is the setting for most of her books.

Many critics have lauded the tetralogy of her New England novels, loosely called "The Incredible Tales" — which consist of *Silky, The Enchanted, Mountain Bride*, and *The White Room* — as her best work, with their lyric descriptions of the deep forests of the New England countryside. The people and cultures of the region are warmly brought to life in stories that combine New Englanders' common sense with the feeling of entering a modern legend.

Born in Buffalo, New York, Coatsworth was educated at Los Robles School in Pasadena, California. Then she came back to the Northeast to study at Buffalo Seminary and Vassar College in Poughkeepsie, New York, where she received her B.A., and Columbia University, where she received her M.A. She married noted author Henry Beston in 1929 and raised two daughters with him until his death in 1968.

She was the author of over one hundred books of poetry, short stories, and novels for both children and adults.

◆ ◆ ◆

Walter D. Edmonds (1903-1998) claimed that he never really wrote books for children, but rather books for adults and children who like to read. His first novel, *The Matchlock Gun*, a story about frontier survival in America during the 18th century, won the Newbery Medal in 1942. He was fond of using the Boonville area of the Mohawk Valley in New York as a setting for his novels, and one of them, *Bert Breen's Barn*, won the National Book Award and the Christopher Award in 1976.

Edmonds wrote about strong characters who are determined to succeed despite the obstacles they must face. He wrote more than twenty-five novels, including the famous *Drums along the Mohawk*, another account of America as it struggled to expand into the frontier.

Born in Boonville, New York, he studied at Harvard University and later returned there to take a position on the Board of Overseers. He lived in Concord, Massachusetts, until his death.

◆ ◆ ◆

Charles Boardman Hawes (1889-1923) had a promising career cut short by his untimely death. Although his books *The Mutineers* and the Newbery-winning *The Dark Frigate* have been characterized as derivative and flawed, many critics agree that he was just beginning to find his literary voice and could have developed into an author of the likes of Robert Louis Stevenson. Besides those novels, he also wrote *The Great Quest*, as well as two books for adults.

Born in Clifton Springs, New York, he was educated in Bangor, Maine, and later studied at Harvard University, where he was a Longfellow fellow. He married Dorothea Cable in 1916, and the couple had two sons. Before turning to writing, he worked as a staff member of the magazines *Youth's Companion* and *Open Road*.

◆ ◆ ◆

Will James (1892-1942) was the cowboy pseudonym for Joseph Ernest Nepthtali Dufault, the author of several collections of cowboy stories, which, along with his western adult novels, made up the majority of his fiction output.

A cowboy and rodeo rider himself, James brought the American West alive in his stories, writing in the idiosyncratic dialect of the range cowboy. His depiction of the relationship between the cowboy and his horse, recreated memorably in the Newbery Medal-winning book *Smoky, the Cowhorse*, published in 1926, resurrected an image of the West that was fast dying out. A large part of what made his books so absorbing were his own illustrations, featuring well-muscled horses in powerful, realistic action scenes.

Unfortunately, his past caught up with him. He served a prison sentence for cattle rustling in 1915 before turning to writing, and later, after he wrote his autobiography, it was discovered by outside authenticators that his written life was almost entirely made up, created out of the cowboy illusions that he wrote, ironically, with such realism.

◆ ◆ ◆

Lois Lenski (1893-1974) is known primarily for her series of middle-school books detailing the lives of everyday American families. Volumes such as *Cotton in My Sack*, *Shoo-Fly Girl*, and *San Francisco Boy*, respectively, detail the fictional lives of a Southern sharecropper girl, a Pennsylvania Amish girl, and a Chinese-American boy living in San Francisco. These books are made all the more real by the author's exhaustive research into the lives of these various regional groups of people, often including visits to see their day-to-day activities in person.

Born in Springfield, Ohio, she earned a B.S. in education from Ohio State University, then went on to study at the Art Students' League in New York and the prestigious Westminster School of Art in London. Right after school, she married the artist Arthur Covey and raised their son and two stepchildren with him until his death in 1960. Her artwork garnered her several single artist shows, notably a display of oil paintings in the Weyhe Gallery and a watercolors show in the Ferargils Gallery, both in New York. She also was included in group art shows at the Pennsylvania Water Color Show and the New York Water Color Show.

During her lifetime, she wrote more than one hundred books of stories, poetry, and plays, the majority of them illustrated by her as well. Her autobiography, *Journey into Childhood*, was finished two years before her death.

◆ ◆ ◆

Elizabeth Yates (1905-   ) is the pseudonym for **Elizabeth Yates McGreal**, who researched and turned the real-life story of a slave in colonial America and his fight to be free into the book *Amos*

Fortune, Free Man, winner of the 1951 Newbery Medal. Besides writing about Amos Fortune, Yates has chronicled the lives of other people who have challenged society, such as Dorothy Canfield Fisher, David Livingstone, and Prudence Crandall, who, in Connecticut in 1833, began the first school to accept European and African-American children on an equal basis.

Courageous characters populate Yates's fiction as well. In *Carolina's Courage*, a young girl's fearlessness and spirit are put to the test when she befriends a little Native American girl. The gifts the two exchange, Carolina's beautiful porcelain doll for the other girl's buffalo hide one, inadvertently save her family from hostile Native Americans.

Writing is a subject dear to Yates's heart, as evidenced by her willingness to speak to school groups in her area, even when she was well into her eighties. She has also written the book *Someday You'll Write*, a primer for children that emphasizes patience, hard work, and perseverance as requirements for success.

Born in Buffalo, New York, Yates married William McGreal, and the two lived in England for a number of years before settling on a New Hampshire farm in 1939. Yates has written and lectured about writing for decades, teaching at various colleges such as the Universities of Connecticut, New Hampshire, and Indiana. She has also instructed at various Christian Writers and Editors conferences and is a Trustee of the Peterborough Town Library in New Hampshire. She has received several honorary degrees, most notably literary degrees from Aurora University, Ripon College, the University of New Hampshire, and Rivier College.

❧ Newbery Award-Winning Books ❧

2000

WINNER:
Bud, Not Buddy by Christopher Paul Curtis

HONOR BOOKS:
Getting Near to Baby
by Audrey Couloumbis

Our Only May Amelia
by Jennifer L. Holm

26 Fairmount Avenue
by Tomie dePaola

1999

WINNER:
Holes by Louis Sachar

HONOR BOOK:
A Long Way from Chicago
by Richard Peck

1998

WINNER:
Out of the Dust by Karen Hesse

HONOR BOOKS:
Ella Enchanted by Gail Carson Levine
Lily's Crossing by Patricia Reilly Giff
Wringer by Jerry Spinelli

1997

WINNER:
The View from Saturday
by E.L. Konigsburg

HONOR BOOKS:
Belle Prater's Boy by Ruth White
A Girl Named Disaster
by Nancy Farmer
Moorchild by Eloise McGraw
The Thief by Megan Whalen Turner

1996

WINNER:
The Midwife's Apprentice
by Karen Cushman

HONOR BOOKS:
The Great Fire by Jim Murphy

*The Watsons Go to
Birmingham — 1963*
by Christopher Paul Curtis

What Jamie Saw by Carolyn Coman

Yolanda's Genius by Carol Fenner

1995

WINNER:
Walk Two Moons
by Sharon Creech

HONOR BOOKS:
Catherine, Called Birdy
by Karen Cushman

The Ear, the Eye, and the Arm
by Nancy Farmer

1994

WINNER:
The Giver by Lois Lowry

HONOR BOOKS:
Crazy Lady by Jane Leslie Conly

Dragon's Gate by Laurence Yep

*Eleanor Roosevelt:
A Life of Discovery*
by Russell Freedman

1993

WINNER:
Missing May by Cynthia Rylant

HONOR BOOKS:
*The Dark-thirty: Southern
Tales of the Supernatural*
by Patricia McKissack

Somewhere in the Darkness
by Walter Dean Myers

What Hearts by Bruce Brooks

1992

WINNER:
Shiloh by Phyllis Reynolds Naylor

HONOR BOOKS:
Nothing But the Truth:
A Documentary Novel
by Avi

The Wright Brothers: How They
Invented the Airplane
by Russell Freedman

1991

WINNER:
Maniac Magee by Jerry Spinelli

HONOR BOOK:
The True Confessions of
Charlotte Doyle
by Avi

1990

WINNER:
Number the Stars by Lois Lowry

HONOR BOOKS:
Afternoon of the Elves
by Janet Taylor Lisle

Shabanu Daughter
of the Wind
by Suzanne Fisher Staples

The Winter Room by Gary Paulsen

1989

WINNER:
Joyful Noise: Poems for Two Voices
by Paul Fleischman

HONOR BOOKS:
In the Beginning: Creation Stories
from around the World
by Virginia Hamilton

Scorpions by Walter Dean Myers

1988

WINNER:
Lincoln: A Photobiography
by Russell Freedman

HONOR BOOKS:
After the Rain
by Norma Fox Mazer

Hatchet by Gary Paulsen

1987

WINNER:
The Whipping Boy by Sid Fleischman

HONOR BOOKS:
A Fine White Dust by Cynthia Rylant

On My Honor by Marion Dane Bauer

Volcano: The Eruption and
Healing of Mount St. Helens
by Patricia Lauber

1986

WINNER:
Sarah, Plain and Tall
by Patricia MacLachlan

HONOR BOOKS:
Commodore Perry in the
Land of the Shogun
by Rhonda Blumberg

Dogsong by Gary Paulsen

1985

WINNER:
The Hero and the Crown
by Robin McKinley

HONOR BOOKS:
Like Jake and Me by Mavis Jukes

The Moves Make the Man
by Bruce Brooks

One-Eyed Cat by Paula Fox

1984

WINNER:
Dear Mr. Henshaw by Beverly Cleary

HONOR BOOKS:
The Sign of the Beaver
by Elizabeth George Speare

A Solitary Blue by Cynthia Voigt

Sugaring Time by Kathryn Lasky

The Wish Giver: Three
Tales of Coven Tree
by Bill Brittain

1983

WINNER:
Dicey's Song by Cynthia Voigt

HONOR BOOKS:

The Blue Sword by Robin McKinley

Doctor DeSoto by William Steig

Graven Images by Paul Fleischman

Homesick: My Own Story by Jean Fritz

Sweet Whispers, Brother Rush
by Virginia Hamilton

1982

WINNER:

*A Visit to William Blake's Inn:
Poems for Innocent and
Experienced Travelers*
by Nancy Willard

HONOR BOOKS:

Ramona Quimby, Age 8
by Beverly Cleary

*Upon the Head of the Goat: A
Childhood in Hungary 1939-1944*
by Aranka Siegal

1981

WINNER:

Jacob Have I Loved
by Katherine Paterson

HONOR BOOKS:

The Fledgling by Jane Langton

A Ring of Endless Light
by Madeleine L'Engle

1980

WINNER:

*A Gathering of Days: A New England
Girl's Journal, 1830-1832*
by Joan W. Blos

HONOR BOOK:

*The Road from Home: The
Story of an Armenian Girl*
by David Kherdian

1979

WINNER:

The Westing Game by Ellen Raskin

HONOR BOOK:

The Great Gilly Hopkins
by Katherine Paterson

1978

WINNER:

Bridge to Terabithia
by Katherine Paterson

HONOR BOOKS:

Anpao: An American Indian Odyssey
by Jamake Highwater

Ramona and Her Father
by Beverly Cleary

1977

WINNER:

Roll of Thunder, Hear My Cry
by Mildred D. Taylor

HONOR BOOKS:

Abel's Island by William Steig

A String in the Harp by Nancy Bond

1976

WINNER:

The Grey King by Susan Cooper

HONOR BOOKS:

Dragonwings by Laurence Yep

The Hundred Penny Box
by Sharon Bell Mathis

1975

WINNER:

M.C. Higgins, the Great
by Virginia Hamilton

HONOR BOOKS:

Figgs & Phantoms by Ellen Raskin

My Brother Sam Is Dead
by James Lincoln Collier
and Christopher Collier

The Perilous Gard
by Elizabeth Marie Pope

Philip Hall Likes Me, I Reckon Maybe
by Bette Greene

1974

WINNER:

The Slave Dancer by Paula Fox

HONOR BOOK:

The Dark Is Rising by Susan Cooper

1973

WINNER:
Julie of the Wolves
by Jean Craighead George

HONOR BOOKS:
Frog and Toad Together
by Arnold Lobel

The Upstairs Room by Johanna Reiss

The Witches of Worm
by Zilpha Keatley Snyder

1972

WINNER:
Mrs. Frisby and the Rats of NIMH
by Robert C. O'Brien

HONOR BOOKS:
Annie and the Old One
by Miska Miles

The Headless Cupid
by Zilpha Keatley Snyder

Incident at Hawk's Hill
by Allan W. Eckert

The Planet of Junior Brown
by Virginia Hamilton

The Tombs of Atuan
by Ursula K. Le Guin

1971

WINNER:
Summer of the Swans by Betsy Byars

HONOR BOOKS:
Enchantress from the Stars
by Sylvia Louise Engdahl

Knee Knock Rise by Natalie Babbitt

Sing Down the Moon by Scott O'Dell

1970

WINNER:
Sounder by William H. Armstrong

HONOR BOOKS:
Journey Outside by Mary Q. Steele

*The Many Ways of Seeing: An
Introduction to the Pleasures of Art*
by Janet Gaylord Moore

Our Eddie by Sulamith Ish-Kishor

1969

WINNER:
The High King by Lloyd Alexander

HONOR BOOKS:
To Be a Slave by Julius Lester

*When Shlemiel Went to Warsaw
and Other Stories*
by Isaac Bashevis Singer

1968

WINNER:
*From the Mixed-Up Files of
Mrs. Basil E. Frankweiler*
by E.L. Konigsburg

HONOR BOOKS:
The Black Pearl
by Scott O'Dell

The Egypt Game
by Zilpha Keatley Snyder

The Fearsome Inn
by Isaac Bashevis Singer

*Jennifer, Hecate, Macbeth, William
McKinley, and Me, Elizabeth*
by E.L. Konigsburg

1967

WINNER:
Up a Road Slowly by Irene Hunt

HONOR BOOKS:
The Jazz Man by Mary Hays Weik

The King's Fifth by Scott O'Dell

*Zlateh the Goat and
Other Stories*
by Isaac Bashevis Singer

1966

WINNER:
I, Juan de Pareja
by Elizabeth Borton de Trevino

HONOR BOOKS:
The Animal Family
by Randall Jarrell

The Black Cauldron
by Lloyd Alexander

The Noonday Friends by Mary Stolz

1965

WINNER:
Shadow of a Bull
by Maia Wojciechowska

HONOR BOOK:
Across Five Aprils by Irene Hunt

1964

WINNER:
It's Like This, Cat by Emily Neville

HONOR BOOKS:
The Loner by Ester Wier

Rascal: A Memoir of a Better Era
by Sterling North

1963

WINNER:
A Wrinkle in Time
by Madeleine L'Engle

HONOR BOOKS:
Men of Athens by Olivia Coolidge

*Thistle and Thyme: Tales and
Legends from Scotland*
by Sorche Nic Leodhas

1962

WINNER:
The Bronze Bow
by Elizabeth George Speare

HONOR BOOKS:
Belling the Tiger by Mary Stolz

Frontier Living by Edwin Tunis

The Golden Goblet
by Eloise Jarvis McGraw

1961

WINNER:
Island of the Blue Dolphins
by Scott O'Dell

HONOR BOOKS:
*America Moves Forward:
A History for Peter*
by Gerald W. Johnson

The Cricket in Times Square
by George Selden

Old Ramon by Jack Schaefer

1960

WINNER:
Onion John by Joseph Krumgold

HONOR BOOKS:
*American Is Born:
A History for Peter*
by Gerald W. Johnson

The Gammage Cup by Carol Kendall

My Side of the Mountain
by Jean Craighead George

1959

WINNER:
The Witch of Blackbird Pond
by Elizabeth George Speare

HONOR BOOKS:
Along Came a Dog
by Meindert DeJong

Chucaro: Wild Pony of the Pampa
by Francis Kalnay

The Family Under the Bridge
by Natalie Savage Carlson

The Perilous Road by William O. Steele

1958

WINNER:
Rifles for Watie by Harold Keith

HONOR BOOKS:
Gone-Away Lake by Elizabeth Enright

The Great Wheel by Robert Lawson

The Horsecatcher by Mari Sandoz

Tom Paine, Freedom's Apostle
by Leo Gurko

1957

WINNER:
Miracles on Maple Hill
by Virginia Sorenson

HONOR BOOKS:
Black Fox of Lorne
by Marguerite de Angeli

The Corn Grows Ripe
by Dorothy Rhoads

The House of Sixty Fathers
by Meindert DeJong

Mr. Justice Holmes
by Clara Ingram Judson

Old Yeller by Fred Gipson

1956

WINNER:
Carry On, Mr. Bowditch
by Jean Lee Latham

HONOR BOOKS:
The Golden Name Day
by Jennie Lindquist

Men, Microscopes, and Living Things
by Katherine Shippen

The Secret River
by Marjorie Kinnan Rawlings

1955

WINNER:
The Wheel on the School
by Meindert DeJong

HONOR BOOKS:
Banner in the Sky by James Ullman

Courage of Sarah Noble
by Alice Dalgliesh

1954

WINNER:
. . . And Now Miguel
by Joseph Krumgold

HONOR BOOKS:
All Alone by Claire Huchet Bishop

Hurry Home, Candy
by Meindert DeJong

Magic Maize by Mary and Conrad Buff

Shadrach by Meindert DeJong

Theodore Roosevelt, Fighting Patriot
by Clara Ingram Judson

1953

WINNER:
Secret of the Andes
by Ann Nolan Clark

HONOR BOOKS:
The Bears on Hemlock Mountain
by Alice Dalgliesh

Birthdays of Freedom, Vol. 1
by Genevieve Foster

Charlotte's Web by E.B. White

Moccasin Trail by Eloise McGraw

Red Sails to Capri by Ann Weil

1952

WINNER:
Ginger Pye by Eleanor Estes

HONOR BOOKS:
Americans Before Columbus
by Elizabeth Baity

The Apple and the Arrow
by Mary and Conrad Buff

The Defender by Nicholas Kalashnikoff

The Light at Tern Rock by Julia Sauer

Minn of the Mississippi
by Holling C. Holling

1951

WINNER:
Amos Fortune, Free Man
by Elizabeth Yates

HONOR BOOKS:
Abraham Lincoln, Friend
of the People
by Clara Ingram Judson

Better Known as Johnny Appleseed
by Mabel Leigh Hunt

Gandhi, Fighter without a Sword
by Jeanette Eaton

The Story of Appleby Capple
by Anne Parrish

1950

WINNER:
The Door in the Wall
by Marguerite de Angeli

HONOR BOOKS:
The Blue Cat of Castle Town
by Catherine Coblentz

George Washington
by Genevieve Foster

Kildee House
by Rutherford Montgomery

*Song of the Pines: A Story of
Norwegian Lumbering in Wisconsin*
by Walter and Marion Havighurst

Tree of Freedom by Rebecca Caudill

1949

WINNER:
King of the Wind by Marguerite Henry

HONOR BOOKS:
Daughter of the Mountain
by Louise Rankin

My Father's Dragon by Ruth S. Gannett

Seabird by Holling C. Holling

Story of the Negro by Arna Bontemps

1948

WINNER:
The Twenty-One Balloons
by William Pène du Bois

HONOR BOOKS:
*The Cow-Tail Switch, and
Other West African Stories*
by Harold Courlander

Li Lun, Lad of Courage
by Carolyn Treffinger

Misty of Chincoteague
by Marguertie Henry

Pancakes-Paris
by Claire Huchet Bishop

*The Quaint and Curious Quest
of Johnny Longfoot*
by Catherine Besterman

1947

WINNER:
Miss Hickory by Carolyn Sherwin Bailey

HONOR BOOKS:
The Avion My Uncle Flew
by Cyrus Fisher

Big Tree by Mary and Conrad Buff

The Heavenly Tenants
by William Maxwell

The Hidden Treasure of Glaston
by Eleanor Jewett

Wonderful Year by Nancy Barnes

1946

WINNER:
Strawberry Girl by Lois Lenski

HONOR BOOKS:
Bhimsa, the Dancing Bear
by Christine Weston

Justin Morgan Had a Horse
by Marguerite Henry

The Moved-Outers
by Florence Crannell Means

New Found World
by Katherine Shippen

1945

WINNER:
Rabbit Hill by Robert Lawson

HONOR BOOKS:
Abraham Lincoln's World
by Genevieve Foster

The Hundred Dresses
by Eleanor Estes

*Lone Journey: The Life of
Roger Williams*
by Jeanette Eaton

The Silver Pencil by Alice Dalgliesh

1944

WINNER:
Johnny Tremain by Esther Forbes

HONOR BOOKS:
Fog Magic by Julia Sauer

Mountain Born by Elizabeth Yates

Rufus M. by Eleanor Estes

These Happy Golden Years
by Laura Ingalls Wilder

1943

WINNER:
Adam of the Road
by Elizabeth Janet Gray

HONOR BOOKS:
Have You Seen Tom Thumb?
by Mabel Leigh Hunt

The Middle Moffat by Eleanor Estes

1942

WINNER:
The Matchlock Gun
by Walter D. Edmonds

HONOR BOOKS:
Down Ryton Water by Eva Roe Gaggin

George Washington's World
by Genevieve Foster

*Indian Captive: The Story
of Mary Jemison*
by Lois Lenski

Little Town on the Prairie
by Laura Ingalls Wilder

1941

WINNER:
Call It Courage by Armstrong Sperry

HONOR BOOKS:
Blue Willow by Doris Gates

The Long Winter
by Laura Ingalls Wilder

Nansen by Anna Gertrude Hall

Young Mac of Fort Vancouver
by Mary Jane Carr

1940

WINNER:
Daniel Boone by James Daugherty

HONOR BOOKS:
Boy with a Pack by Stephen W. Meader

By the Shores of Silver Lake
by Laura Ingalls Wilder

*Runner of the Mountain Tops:
The Life of Louis Agassiz*
by Mabel Robinson

The Singing Tree by Kate Seredy

1939

WINNER:
Thimble Summer by Elizabeth Enright

HONOR BOOKS:
Hello the Boat! by Phyllis Crawford

*Leader by Destiny: George
Washington, Man and Patriot*
by Jeanette Eaton

Mr. Popper's Penguins
by Richard and Florence Atwater

Nino by Valenti Angelo

Penn by Elizabeth Janet Gray

1938

WINNER:
The White Stag by Kate Seredy

HONOR BOOKS:
Bright Island by Mabel Robinson

On the Banks of Plum Creek
by Laura Ingalls Wilder

Pecos Bill by James Cloyd Bowman

1937

WINNER:
Roller Skates by Ruth Sawyer

HONOR BOOKS:
Audubon by Constance Rourke

The Codfish Musket by Agnes Hewes

The Golden Basket
by Ludwig Bemelmans

Phoebe Fairchild: Her Book
by Lois Lenski

Whistler's Van by Idwal Jones

Winterbound by Margery Bianco

1936

WINNER:
Caddie Woodlawn by Carol Ryrie Brink

HONOR BOOKS:
*All Sail Set: A Romance of
the Flying Cloud*
by Armstrong Sperry

The Good Master by Kate Seredy

Honk, the Moose by Phil Stong

Young Walter Scott
by Elizabeth Janet Gray

1935

WINNER:
Dobry by Monica Shannon

HONOR BOOKS:
Davy Crockett by Constance Rourke

*Days on Skates: The Story
of a Dutch Picnic*
by Hilda Von Stockum

Pageant of Chinese History
by Elizabeth Seeger

1934

WINNER:
*Invincible Louisa: The Story
of the Author of* Little Women
by Cornelia Meigs

HONOR BOOKS:
ABC Bunny by Wanda Gág

Apprentice of Florence by Ann Kyle

*Big Tree of Bunlahy: Stories
of My Own Countryside*
by Padraic Colum

The Forgotten Daughter
by Caroline Snedeker

Glory of the Seas by Agnes Hewes

New Land by Sarah Schmidt

Swords of Steel
by Elsie Singmaster

Winged Girl of Knossos
by Erik Berry

1933

WINNER:
Young Fu of the Upper Yangtze
by Elizabeth Lewis

HONOR BOOKS:
*Children of the Soil: A
Story of Scandinavia*
by Nora Burglon

*The Railroad to Freedom:
A Story of the Civil War*
by Hildegarde Swift

Swift Rivers by Cornelia Meigs

1932

WINNER:
Waterless Mountain
by Laura Adams Armer

HONOR BOOKS:
Boy of the South Seas
by Eunice Tietjens

Calico Bush by Rachel Field

The Fairy Circus by Dorothy P. Lathrop

Jane's Island by Marjorie Allee

Out of the Flame by Eloise Lownsbery

*Truce of the Wolf and Other
Tales of Old Italy*
by Mary Gould Davis

1931

WINNER:
The Cat Who Went to Heaven
by Elizabeth Coatsworth

HONOR BOOKS:
*The Dark Star of Itza: The
Story of a Pagan Princess*
by Alida Malkus

Floating Island by Anne Parrish

*Garram the Hunter: A Boy
of the Hill Tribes*
by Herbert Best

Meggy Macintosh
by Elizabeth Janet Gray

Mountains Are Free
by Julia Davis Adams

Ood-Le-Uk the Wanderer
by Alice Lide and Margaret Johansen

Queer Person by Ralph Hubbard

Spice and the Devil's Cake
by Agnes Hewes

1930

WINNER:
Hitty, Her First Hundred Years
by Rachel Field

HONOR BOOKS:
*A Daughter of the Seine: The
Life of Madam Roland*
by Jeanette Eaton

Jumping-Off Place
by Marian Hurd McNeely

Little Blacknose by Hildegarde Swift

Pran of Albania by Elizabeth Miller

*The Tangle-Coated Horse
and Other Tales*
by Ella Young

Vaino by Julia Davis Adams

1929

WINNER:
The Trumpeter of Krakow
by Eric P. Kelly

HONOR BOOKS:
The Boy Who Was by Grace Hallock
Clearing Weather by Cornelia Meigs
Millions of Cats by Wanda Gág
Pigtail of Ah Lee Ben Loo
by John Bennett
Runaway Papoose by Grace Moon
Tod of the Fens by Elinor Whitney

1928

WINNER:
Gay Neck, the Story of a Pigeon
by Dhan Gopal Mukerji

HONOR BOOKS:
Downright Dencey
by Caroline Snedeker
The Wonder Smith and His Son
by Ella Young

1927

WINNER:
Smoky, the Cowhorse by Will James

1926

WINNER:
Shen of the Sea
by Arthur Bowie Chrisman

HONOR BOOK:
*The Voyagers: Being Legends and
Romances of Atlantic Discovery*
by Padraic Colum

1925

WINNER:
Tales from Silver Lands
by Charles Finger

HONOR BOOKS:
The Dream Coach by Anne Parrish
*Nicholas: A Manhattan
Christmas Story*
by Annie Carroll Moore

1924

WINNER:
The Dark Frigate
by Charles Boardman Hawes

1923

WINNER:
The Voyages of Doctor Doolittle
by Hugh Lofting

1922

WINNER:
The Story of Mankind
by Hendrik Willem van Loon

HONOR BOOKS:
Cedric the Forester
by Bernard Marshall
*The Golden Fleece and the Heroes
Who Lived Before Achilles*
by Padraic Colum
The Great Quest
by Charles Boardman Hawes
*The Old Tobacco Shop: A True
Account of What Befell a Little
Boy in Search of Adventure*
by William Bowen
The Windy Hill by Cornelia Meigs

160